ODDS
&
ENDS

Written by Sean D. Gardner

Edited by Shardae Rudel

ISBN 9798632338479

First printing: May 2020

True Sentence Publishing

To my father and his everlasting memory

Table of contents

The race

The antics of kids will never change. You go out at sunup and make sure you are home before the streetlights come on, "or else," my mom would say. There was nothing quite the same about being a kid, and now looking back at them I feel like an alien. I know I was one, but the real world has stripped me of my innocence. My fully developed brain and conscious keep me from doing stupid things, and pain is now a real thing. There is one time I will always remember though, the time before phones, before HD video games—the day of the neighborhood race.

I remember it was one of those warm summer days where you weren't sweating through your shirt thanks to the breeze. It was one of those perfect days you would hope for as a kid. "Smooth" by Santana and Rob Thomas was on every radio station, and the 7-Eleven was running out of the true lifeline for us kids—The Slurpee. I lived in your typical

Midwestern suburb. All the houses matched, and nothing ever happened, unless you were a kid. I lived behind a school that had a bus circle that us kids would use as a racetrack. You may have heard of the Michigan Motor Speedway or the Indianapolis Motor Speedway, but those do not compare to the Kid-Powered Speedway. In hindsight, it is just a lame circle with jet-black pavement and a grass island in the middle. But as kids, it was *the* hot spot. The island in the middle was full of lemonade stands, snack bars and kids of all ages racing Big Wheels, tricycles, and bicycles. It was amazing to have so much organization at such a young age. We had it all broken down by age group, type of cycle, and who was last in line for the snack bar when the sun went down the day before. This summer was a little different though. Someone made trophies. We were all ecstatic, finally our accomplishments on the racetrack would be noticed and we would forever be known as champions of the **KPS**.

I was seven, going on eight at the time. I'd compare myself to James Dean; I was a rebel without a cause and lived for the racetrack. I had it all, including a red jacket and dark Levi jeans with the bottoms rolled up (my mom bought them big because I'd grow into them). I would put my aviators on, and slick back my golden hair. For a seven-year-old, I looked suave and cool. But what made me look extra cool was my whip. It was a Batman Big Wheel without the noise maker. Being the rebellious James Dean that I was, I found a way to cut off the noise maker, making everyone jealous. It was light blue with a yellow plastic seat and yellow handlebars. The spokes were covered with Batman doing superhero things, and the rear wheels had the bat symbol on them. When I sat in it, I felt like a superhero.

I rolled up from my backyard onto the speedway and I said hi to all the guys, and gave the girls a nasty look. I couldn't have cooties at a time like this. My race was at noon against my biggest rival and best friend Chris. We went way back. We both loved *Star Wars* and soccer. He always dressed up like a little schoolboy in tan pleated pants and a sweater vest. We were the best of pals, always getting in trouble with our parents, whether it was super-soaking beehives or having brutal lightsaber fights. But on race day, there was no such thing as "being friends." We gave each other the death stare and put our thumbs to our nose in an attempt to taunt the other and throw them off their game.

I polished off my Big Wheel before I walked over to the snack bar. When I got there, they had ice-cold pink lemonade. I paid the man twenty-five cents and drank the best summer drink there was. Then my worst nightmare came true, Carly came over. I tried my best to hide by jumping over the snack bar and hiding behind a tree, but it was too late. She saw me and made sure I knew it. In a high-pitched voice that only she could do, she screamed "I see you behind that tree, silly, you can't hide from me." Caught red-handed, I moved my way from the tree but made sure she couldn't get within arm's reach of me. "I just want to wish you good luck, silly." Sometimes I wonder if she thought my name was Silly. Stupidly, I let my guard down and told her OK. With my defense down she attacked me, hugged me like a boa constrictor and gave me a sloppy wet kiss on my cheek. I must have turned to stone, my body turned white as paper and my mouth fell to the ground. I'm dead, I thought. It was a good seven years. *Here lays Harry, death by cooties,* my gravestone would say. I started to feel lightheaded. I finally was able to pry her off me and, still fearing for my life, I was in desperate need for advice. Has anyone even survived cooties before? I found the oldest kid I could find and asked him for his wisdom. He laughed in my face when I told him I was going to die because a girl kissed me. He gave me a high five and told me I was the man. I started to back away slowly and then took off at a full sprint and thought he must be in stage two of cooties because he is delirious.

It was race time, but I had no idea if I would even make it to the end of the race. My face sweating, my perfectly groomed hair was falling all over the place. I was a mess. I nervously rode my Big Wheel to the start line. I whispered to Chris, "Dude, Carly kissed me, and I think I have cooties." He yelled back, "Trying to get into my head? It won't work."

"I'm not joking," I told him, but by then I was talking to the hand and, as you know, the face don't want to hear it. To make my day worse, Carly was the girl who had to wave the start flag. All I thought was who did she share her cookies with to get that job. She blew me a kiss before she said the rules. It was a twelve-lap race. First one to break the tape wins. This of course was standard.

Looking around, there was a sea of people for this race of the century. Two friends pitted in a life or death situation, and a trophy was on the line. Not even the cartoons could think of a better scenario. I was seeing double, the cooties must have hit me hard, so I asked for a five-minute delay. I told the judges that it was for a potty break and my house was just on the other side of the gate. I ran into the house and thankfully there was my dad, sitting in his robe drinking his tea and reading the paper. I jumped on him. Crying, I told him how I was going to die of cooties and on the day of the big race! That's when he told me some mind-blowing stuff. He told me that girls were not evil, and a kiss would not kill you. In fact, he told me, a kiss from a girl before a race gives you the extra strength to win. My dad wouldn't lie to me, so I picked myself up by my bootstraps and, with my confidence restored, fixed my hair and strutted my way out of the house and back onto the racetrack. It was on.

Back in the driver's seat I looked over at Chris and gave him a menacing smile. I saw Carly ready to start the race. I pulled my glasses down and gave her a wink. As soon as I did, she melted to the ground. The older kid was right. I *was* the man. The judges, by this time, were fed up with these delays, and told her to wave the flag to start the race. As I rode toward the first corner, my Big Wheel slid like butter. Everything was going to plan. I was winning by a few feet and the laps just flew by. And then on the tenth lap everything changed. I took a corner a little too inside and hit the curb. I flew off the big wheel and slid for what seemed like miles. I got up, holding back the tears and I noticed a tear in my jacket. Chris stopped to a screeching halt and put his thumb to his nose and sped off without asking if I was OK. There are no yellow flags in the KPS so the race went on. The rage came through me. I ran to my Big Wheel and got back on. Now I was pedaling faster than I ever had before.

We were neck and neck going into the last two laps. We pulled some dirty tricks, pushing at each other and running into each other's Big Wheel. On the last turn of the last lap we both slid, our Big Wheels gliding across the pavement with the finishing tape in our view. We both gave it our all, channeling our inner Luke Skywalker and used our hopefully real Jedi powers to focus and win. I kicked at Chris one more time and it made him lose speed as he regained control. I ripped through the tape and the race was mine. I took an extra slow victory lap and used this opportunity to wave to the crowd and listen to them chant my name.

I was handed the trophy and I held it above my head for all to see. It was the nicest plastic you could find. It had a bike painted in gold on top and a blue tortoise shell shaft. On the base was engraved one word—*winner.* Yes, I was, I thought. I had won the race of the century, and I owed it all to one person. I found Carly and led her to the winner's circle. It was time to celebrate. I took a bottle of pop, shook it up, and sprayed it all over like a real champion. Then I took a glass of milk and chugged it, making sure to leave a manly milk moustache. Finally, I looked over at Carly and with everyone looking at me I gave her the world's fastest kiss, and told her thanks for the extra strength to win. Chris came up to me next and we hugged it out. We were best friends through and through. We spent the next hour talking about all the awesome things we did and how he would have me next time—he never did. The sun started to set so Chris, Carly, and I made our way to my house together for the first time, but certainly not the last.

The three of us have not done much growing up. Chris and I are still as competitive as ever, but thumb-to-the-nose has now become a full-fledged middle finger. Winning the race was my proudest moment and still is. Not for the trophy that's gathering dust in the attic, or the respect of the neighborhood (although I still rub it in Chris's face twenty years later). Carly and I have been inseparable ever since. We will sit in the park and talk about the race and how "we" began, pointing out the kids that remind of us of our younger days. I have learned a lot from my dad but finding out cooties only help you has been the most important. Although I should have paid more attention to the "how to fix your house" talk.

A journey home

He walked back into his room and took a silent look around. It was familiar, yet strange to him. Posters of his favorite sports teams lined the walls, his trophies of past accomplishments gathered dust on the dresser and his bed sat freshly made, ready for him to ruin. It had hardly changed since he left two years ago. His bag slipped off his shoulder and landed with a muffled punch on the floor. The bed hissed an awful screech as he sat down and his eyes were immediately drawn to the gold lettering inscribed on his pack. It read *Lieutenant Michael Taylor.*

He sat stiff in his own room. Although he knew the place he called home for eighteen years, he moved around like he was in a museum. He kept his hands close to his sides as he looked at his own belongings. Each step he took was gingerly and very thought out, as if creaking a floorboard was a crime.

When he caught his eye in the mirror he stopped and shuttered.

Michael came to attention and clicked his boots. He was a well-built man, yet slender, having missed a few meals over the last two years. His brown hair was messily combed over to the side and dull. His skin was a creamy white, like an old cup of coffee, but for the drooping black bags under his eyes of a man desperate for sleep. His large hands were dirty. Each fingernail mangled and broken, painted with a mix of blood and mud that settled underneath each nail.

The closet door was gently pulled open and inside he found a pair of blue jeans and a flannel shirt. He neatly folded his uniform and laid it on the bed. The aches and pains shot up and down his body as he pulled the pants up and over the stitches on his knee and he winced as he pulled his shirt down on his badly bruised body.

"Oh, Michael," Mrs. Taylor said, walking into his room. "Those old clothes are just hanging off of you."

He half smiled and shrugged back at his mom. "It's OK, I guess."

She looked him up and down and nearly shrieked at all the dirt on his fingers.

"Let's get you washed up and I'll make you a big hearty meal," she said before kissing her son on the forehead.

"We will get those pants fitting properly in no time."

She grabbed at his arm as Michael started down the stairs. She noticed a newfound limp on her son and dug her nails into his arm as she held back tears.

"Ma, it's OK," he said. "These aren't the first stairs I've battled since being discharged."

She gave out a nervous laugh and hesitantly loosened her

grip as mothers often do.

Michael gripped the banister and looked around the house. He noticed old pictures of his younger smiling self and the traditional family portraits from Christmastime.

"Your father should be home soon," he heard behind his thoughts like a voice in the distance. He wasn't particularly hungry, he learned to fight the call for hunger on the front but he'd do anything for his mom and if he was being honest with himself, he did miss her homemade pasta. Even her worst meal was better than the rations he forced down.

At first he twirled his fork aimlessly in the bowl and pushed around the noodles like he was a kid hiding his vegetables to earn his dessert. He caught his mom's pale-stricken gaze that made her red lipstick stick out like a sore thumb and scarfed down the plate. Almost immediately she scooped another generous helping on his plate.

"Mom, really, I'm not that hungry. I ate before I got home—honest."

"I know, Michael, but I just worry. I haven't seen you for years and I'm worried you didn't eat too well. Who knows what they have all the way over there."

Michael rolled his eyes and tried to think of a snarky remark, but before he could his dad came storming through the door.

"Son, welcome home," he said behind a waterfall of tears. He grabbed his boy up from the chair, counted his limbs, eyes, ears, fingers and toes and gave him a hug that cracked his son's back.

"At least you came back in one piece," Mr. Taylor chuckled.

"You bet, Dad."

"I'll make you a plate, dear, let Michael get back to eating," Mrs. Taylor said. "He lost too much weight over there."

Michael's mood started to lift and for a moment he felt like he was truly back home. He laughed, made jokes, and caught up with his parents. His face started to hurt from smiling so much at once, a rarity in the last two years.

A silence overcame the dinner table and his mom put the final dishes into the sink. He felt a tight grip deep inside him. He found it hard to breathe and started to feel a cold sweat on his brow. He gripped the table and avoided all eye contact as his mind began to race. Explosions rang in his head, the screams of his friends and the pitter-patter of bullets flying into the ground drowned out his parents. He took a few deep breaths and listened to his heartbeat through his chest.

Calm down, Mike, he told himself. You're home. You're home. You're home.

Tires screeched outside and an engine roared down the street. Mike sprang up out of his chair, knocking it over, and screamed.

"It's OK, Son, it's just the dumbass neighbor and their race car," Mr. Taylor said. "If I've told him once, I've told him hundred times to knock that shit out."

He reached for his kid and placed his hand comfortably on his shoulder. "Look here, boy. You're home now. It's going to be OK."

He looked over to his wife, who could no longer hold the tears back.

"You just gotta get re-accustomed, Mike."

Michael felt his dad's hand on his shoulder and the nightmares disappeared and his heart started to beat normally.

"I think I ought to head to bed. It's been an eventful day," Michael said. "It will probably be good for me."

A week went by and every day was the same. He tossed and turned in bed and woke up in a puddle of sweat stained into his sheets. Screams filled his head and then came out of his mouth. His parents rushed in and saw their boy in tears. Along with the bad was the good. He laughed, watched sports with his dad, and sipped on whiskey, but when the memories came all was lost. Even the smallest noises set him off. Racoons rummaged on trash day and his eyes shot open and he nervously checked the window gripping a knife from his pack. When he was sure it was safe, he'd crawl back into bed holding the knife under his pillow, never parting with it until the sun rose.

One morning he ventured into town. It was the first time his mother let him leave the house since coming home. He breathed in the fresh air and a sudden calmness came over him. A calmness he hadn't felt since before he came home.

Once in town the nerves got the best of him.

"It's just people, Mike. People you've known your whole life," he told himself.

As he walked men tipped their caps, stopped and shook his hand, and told him thank you. Little boys awed at him and they told their parents they just met a real hero. His body shook as he looked down at them with an awkward smile. His vision started to get blurry and he spun around, running into the nearest storefront to get away and was hit with the smell of fresh bread.

"Well, it could have been worse."

He grabbed a fresh loaf of bread, turned around and immediately dropped the loaf.

"Eek, I didn't mean to startle you," Katie said. "I saw you walking and I just wanted to say it is really good to see you again . . . I was worried I may not."

Mike stared at Katie and felt an anxiety that was worse than any memory of war. He looked her up and down and noticed how much growing she did since he'd been gone. He became awestruck by her flowing blonde hair and piercing blue eyes. Her smile dug into his heart and he almost forgot how to speak.

"Well, it was up in the air there for a while," he said, gaining his confidence back.

"Oh my, are you serious . . . What happened?" she said with instant regret. "I mean, you don't have to answer that. I don't want you to if it doesn't make you comfortable."

"Honestly, I haven't thought about it much," he said with a sore smile. "Can I get you a cup of coffee and we can catch up?"

He held onto his coffee tightly and walked down the cobblestone street with Katie. The brick-and-mortar stores made him feel trapped and the passing cars made him jump.

"You seem a bit antsy, Mike," she said. "Do you want to sit down?"

"You know, it's odd. I never expected to be like this," he said as they made their way to a bench. "Everyone stops and says 'thank you' and even my parents treat me different. I can't sleep and I can't get it out of my head. Funny enough, the only time I've felt fine is when I'm alone again."

"Well maybe you should go away for a bit and find

yourself."

He stared into Katie's eyes and thought for a minute. He considered an old camping spot he used to frequent and how the sun beat down on the river and the birds sang their innocent songs.

"You may be onto something there."

"I always knew what was best for you."

"If only I had you by my side over there. I probably wouldn't have gotten into any mess."

Mike told Katie about how he got hurt and ultimately sent home. He told her about being reckless and wanting to be a hero and volunteering for a mission.

"You'll be in and out. As routine as it could be," he remembered the general saying.

It was anything but. After an ambush, he took a bullet to the leg and his squad was left without ammo until they were miraculously saved.

Hours passed by in an instant and Mike took Katie to her door and they said their goodbyes.

"Don't forget what I said, Mike," she said as they held each other. "Get out of here for a while, it will be good for you." She gave him a passionate kiss on the lips and looked up at him. "Hurry back though, I'll be anxious for our next date."

Mike took her advice seriously and thought about the old spot and how he'd break the news to his parents.

The miles of walking began to catch up to him and his knee started throbbing in pain as he approached the door to his home. He grabbed the doorknob and leaned into it and almost toppled to the ground as his mom, who was staring out the window waiting, swung it open.

"I was worried sick about you, Michael. We both were."

"I'm sorry but can I talk to you guys for a second . . . it's important."

They sat down on the couch and Mike broke the news that he had to leave.

"But you just got . . ." his mom began before being cut off by Mr. Taylor.

"I thought as much. It's like you're not really home yet. Just tell us what you need."

Ominous clouds began to fill the sky the next morning, yet Michael pushed on and threw a backpack into the trunk, grabbed the cooler his mom packed with enough food to feed a family for the week—let alone one person camping— and tugged on the straps holding a canoe snuggly on the roof.

Michael drove alone on an old road out of town and watched the traffic backup going into town. The yellow lines were faded on the tattered road littered with potholes. The uneven roadway proved a challenge for any driver who appreciated their vehicle and tires. For miles the car moved slowly, zigging and zagging to avoid danger until he hit the freshly paved turnpike in front of the assembly plant. The building stood like a mighty castle in the concrete jungle of the city. Michael slammed on the brakes and felt a cold shock run down his back as he gazed at the smokestacks spitting out smoke, a line of airplanes ready for use, and billboards asking for war bonds. He stared up at the poster painted in dazzling colors and an eager face running into battle. He lost himself in the eyes of the soldier and began to hear the screams and explosions of the past. The truck's tires squealed and smoke oozed from the pavement as

Michael sped off. He spit out the window and continued his way north, all the while keeping a nervous eye on his rearview mirror and fixated on the plant until it was safely out of sight.

The gray skies followed north and grew darker at the campsite as Michael pulled into an empty stretch of land hugging a river. A few trees were scattered around and provided enough cover from the winds and rains surely on their way. Michael hung a tarp between a handful of trees and placed his tent under it and threw his pack inside and laid down.

After a quick rest he pushed his way up a trailhead and marched through a narrow passage that opened up onto a rocky plateau. The wilderness opened up and he saw the deep valley sprawled out across the land, cut in half by a winding river and enclosed by towering mountains lightly powdered with snow. From the plateau he grew uneasy. The clumps of grey clouds quickly pushed their way across the sky, like huddled bodies at a concert. In the distance wisps of clouds made their way to the ground. The explosions filled his head but he soon realized it was the storm moving quickly towards him. He turned and ran from the sounds and the rain and moved his way back through the wooded trail. He jumped over roots, weaved between tall pines, and crossed over the river via a beaver dam and back into his campsite. He strapped his tent to the tree and huddled himself inside the tent, nearly in tears as the thunder clapped above him and the rain echoed off the tarp above him.

Michael now sat shamelessly in his own tears, screaming at the top of his lungs as the lightning struck. He cursed the war, he cursed God, and he cursed himself. In a fit of rage he brought himself out of the tent and stood in the rainfall and watched the clouds.

"If you won't go, I will!" he screamed to the heavens.

Michael ripped the canoe off the truck and threw it on top of his back and grabbed a paddle. The rain rang off of the aluminum hull and reminded him of bullets glancing off a tank. He plopped it into the water and climbed in. He scanned the sky for any sign of blue or sun shining and caught a beam of light shining down in the distance like a spotlight. Michael dug the paddle through the water and heaved it backwards. The current pushed back and the canoe seemed to stand still in the current. The chains wrapped around Michael's heart and a smog began to fill his head with every clap of thunder and every lightning strike. His shoulders burned, stomach ached, and he couldn't discern between his screams or the ones in his head, but he paddled on.

He remembered being in a freshly washed uniform, thinking how glorious the war would be and how he'd come home with medals and be a hero. He remembered his first mission and being struck with the reality of war, the lies of glory, and the men around him, some of them his closest friends, lying in pools of their own blood.

His hands tightly wound around the paddle and blood dripped down it. The rain masked his tears and the thunder masked his screams as he continued to struggle against the mighty river.

He remembered the humming of planes overhead and out of sight and the whistles of bombs falling through the sky. He remembered them landing and bodies torn to bits and cascading with the rubble in the aftermath.

He remembered storming buildings and smashing faces with the stock of his gun. Dragging soldiers, just like him, to prisons and to an uncertain future.

Michael pleaded for forgiveness as he broke his gaze with the beam of light. He cried out and let the emotions take him over.

"I can't fight anymore," he told himself.

The paddle fell with a clunk inside the boat and he brought his bloody hands to his face and let out a painful cry. The current carried him away, back into the eye of the storm. He stared into the river, occasionally catching his ghastly reflection. A shell of himself remained in the canoe, an empty house that once belonged to a young boy. The campsite passed by and Michael guided his canoe to shore. He made his first strides on land and the rain began to fall easier as he brought the canoe back to solid ground. Michael sat on the edge of the river and felt a sudden sense of calm as he looked downstream. He washed the blood from his hands and watched a cardinal swoop past him and find itself on a bare branch of a pine tree near the ground.

The bright red bird looked at Michael and cocked its head, giving him an odd feeling. The bird reminded him of lost friends and he found a certain comfort from the winged creature. He moved towards it, expecting it to dart away, but the bird was not easily startled. It quickly turned its head with a sudden curiosity as Michael got up and walked over to his pack and got his cooler from the tent. He pulled off chunks from the loaf of bread he bought at the market and tossed it in the bird's direction.

The bird hopped down from the branch and started to peck at the bread.

"I'm sorry," Michael said, wiping away the tears running down his face.

He ate a sandwich and filled his canteen with the river water and filled his empty stomach until he had to undo the top button of his pants. Michael constantly watched the bird pecking at bread and couldn't help but give out a smile. He had his back up against a tree and occasionally looked up at the gray sky with his eyes closed and felt the light sprinkle of rain on his skin. When the sunlight broke out from above him, the cool air slowly became a warm breeze and blew the rainwater from the trees.

The sunlight warmed his skin and he stood up, leaning against a tree until the sun ultimately set. As day turned into night he started a fire, changed into dry clothes, brought his pack to the fire, and peered into its wonderment. The flames danced around and the wood crackled. He saw the faces of his parents and Katie as he lost himself in the flames. He breathed in the camp air and felt at peace—an emotion he thought he lost.

The gold lettering of *Lieutenant Michael Taylor* caught his eye as it flickered off the light. Michael reached into the pack and pulled out a beaten-up leather-bound notebook. He cracked it open and began to flip through his journal entries. In between the covers were stories from the front. Some were happy stories, most were nightmares. As he got to the end of the notebook, he turned to a page titled *Goodbye: My final words*. Michael read it over and over again before tearing it from the notebook and throwing it into the fire. In a flash it was ablaze and he gave out one last sigh of relief before falling asleep to the gentle sounds of the crackling fire.

When the light goes out

The light from a lighthouse shined out onto the sea on a stormy November night. Its beam circled around and around, illuminating the devastating power of the sea. The whitecap waves rose foot after foot and came crashing down with a lionlike roar upon the shore, slowly carving away the land into jagged blades of stone. It was here, amid the thrashing, where the lighthouse operator slept soundly inside a quaint little home next to the tower.

Jonah, as he was called, sat in his rocking chair. It squeaked and creaked ever so gently as he rocked back and forth. Where he sat was just in view of the lamp from the lighthouse and he watched it go round, counting the seconds it took before he could see the light again. Some people have sheep to send themselves to Dreamland, but the old man only needed a good chair and the revolving lamp. In this trancelike state it was no wonder he fell asleep. The weight of his head began to be too much and it fell forward and he was out. His long grey beard supported him just enough to keep him from having a sore neck and the old fishermen's sweater kept him sufficiently warm.

Just when he hooked the big fish of his dreams, a bloodcurdling screech rang out of the radio on the side table next to him. The wailing call cried out but it was only static and the shock sent Jonah falling to the floor. He scrambled to the walkie talkie and it fumbled in his hands before he found and pressed the talk button with his thumb.

"This is Jonah, repeat yourself. Over."

Again, there was only static. He smacked the machine and played with the dials and called again and again. He could feel there was someone on the other end. It was what made Jonah the old reliable lighthouse man. The stuff of legend. His reputation preceded him as the always-trustworthy and go-to guy. He trusted his gut and it always sailed him true, the stories told. He tried once more.

"Hello, hello. This is an emergency frequency, please respond."

The static answered again but as Jonah twitched the dial, he could make out the faintest voice and in a few muffled words he understood the message.

"Out . . . can't . . . port . . . storm . . . towards shore."

Jonah dropped the receiver and twisted his head and looked out the window. Just moments ago he was looking out at the calming light, dreaming fondly of a big fish and sunny days. Now he stood trembling. His face was sunken in and pale like a ghost. He now faced the horror of darkness.

"Don't you do this to me tonight, girl."

He ran from the room and glided down the stairs to the basement with the grace of a cat. He pulled on a string and a single lightbulb turned on. It gave him all the light he needed to move through a maze of boxes and junk the room contained and to the fuse box. He ripped open the panel and started moving his hands up and down the fuses, mumbling the labels to himself, until he found the one that said *ship saver.*

The switch snapped with a mechanical clang as he racked it back and forth. He prayed that was all the work that needed to be done, but before he left the musky room he grabbed a flashlight, a box of matches, and a bright yellow rain coat.

Jonah moved well for someone in their seventies but looked every bit of it. He was nimble, short, and slender. His raggedy beard was so white it was almost a beacon in the dark—aside from the bits of food caught in it. His skin was dark and wrinkled from his years at sea. It looked stiff and ready to crack at any moment but looks can be deceiving. Plainly put, he looked like an old helpless man. The kind that breaks your heart and you want to help across the road, but if you rub him the wrong way he could sure enough chase you down in a frenzy and attack you with combinations of curse words never before fathomed.

When he started up the basement stairs, he had a smile. Something told him it was all OK. His face felt flat once he reached the top stair and peered out the window. Still the unsettling darkness remained. He picked up the radio and called out on all frequencies.

"This is Pointe Palace Lighthouse. She's burnt out, trekking there now. Stay safe and Godspeed, she will be shining again in no time. Over and out."

The old man learned long ago to not wait for the response and threw down the radio. They were usually angry captains cussing him out, or prayers, and he didn't have time for either. He was the answer to the problem and sitting on the radio solved nothing. Under his breath he chuckled and quoted the news he read and saw not too long ago. "The worst string of storms in years," they reported. He burst out laughing at his luck. A hell of a practical joke, he thought. Just his kind of luck that the light would go out now.

Jonah slipped into the bright yellow raincoat and swung open the door. The quaintness of the home was shattered. The wind blew with a fiery whistle and the rain poured down in sheets, smacking him in the face as he leaned his head over and marched forward into the storm. Across the way was the entrance to the lighthouse. His jacket glistened as the rain dripped off him and he found himself under the shelter of the tower. As he searched his pockets for the key to the big steel door, he heard waves crashing down just a few feet away. With a heave he pushed it open and stumbled inside.

Jonah bent over, coughing up rainwater, and caught his breath. He kept his head down and didn't dare look up. He knew a seemingly never-ending spiraling staircase was ahead of him, but he figured ignorance was bliss and although he knew exactly how tall it was, what he couldn't see couldn't hurt him. So, he grabbed the repair kit and spare lightbulbs next to the first step and charged onwards. To his luck, with the light burned out, the whole tower was dark. Jonah relied on feel alone and traversed up the rickety stairs. Each step rang like a chime and with a different tune as the steps got smaller the further up he went. At the first plateau he took a deep breath.

"There's two hundred and fifty-five steps left to the top of the old girl," he recited like he was giving a tour. "Each step more dangerous than the last."

He began to struggle up the old steps with the repair kit in tow and bag of supplies strapped to his back. The space got tighter and tighter and Jonah was glad he stayed so thin over the years. He was always worried he wouldn't be able to squeeze through the last few steps and into the lightroom. He huffed and puffed and slid the box through the opening to the top deck of the house. He heaved over, hands stiff on his knees and caught his breath before feeling an odd sensation. The sound of the storm pierced his ears and was clear as day in what should be a soundproof room. Jonah took the flashlight from the bag and illuminated the area. He took a few steps forward and felt a crunch under his feet. Like a detective he snooped around and concluded a gale of wind must have shattered the glass enclosure and sent a shard into the bulb, causing it to go out. The harsh winter weather November threw at mankind seeped into the room and Jonah took a beating from the wind and rain as he struggled around the broken glass.

"Well, damn you too!" he called out.

He turned out the flashlight and looked about towards the sea. He was certain nothing was wrong. He couldn't see or hear anything, which in this case was a relief. It meant no ships had come to shore and he was saved from the screams of drowning seamen and the crumbling metal on the land.

Jonah then turned his flashlight back on and turned attention to the burnt-out light. He pulled on a glove and reached for the bulb. It was still hot and the filament glowed a deep red. He cleared out the broken glass and inspected around the housing and was soon satisfied there wasn't any other damage to it. He reached for the spare bulb and twisted it tightly into place. The tower erupted. The light blinded Jonah and casted out into the distance and cut through the storm like a knife in warm butter. The engine started to hum and slowly the light went round and round.

He rubbed the blindness out of his eyes and when his sight came back he ran to the rail and peered over the side and looked straight down towards the jagged coast. His instincts stayed true and he saw no wreckage, no flesh, and no fiery destruction. Soon enough the engine was moving at full speed and the light was completing its regular tour of duty. In the distance Jonah could hear the faint sound of horns, bells, and whistles singing out in celebration.

He bellowed in laughter and did a little dance and then Jonah fell to the floor in relief. The adrenaline left his body and his old bones and muscles caught up to him. He rummaged through his bag and pulled out a portable radio. The light kept going round and round and he felt its warmth while he sat so near to it. He couldn't help but smile and listen to the little hum of the engine. Soon enough he was in another fight. This time to keep his eyes open. But just before he began to dream about catching fish again, he tuned his radio and whispered, "This is Pointe Palace. She's shining true. Welcome home."

The fighter

He awoke to a stack of money being dropped on his hand. His outstretched arm ached under the weight of each bill as they landed.

"Done already?" he said, smiling through a fat lip as he watched the money be put back into the safe.

"You did good, kid. You lost, but you did good." The man with the money said.

"He had a good hook, haha. I didn't see it coming. Last thing I remember is a couple of Tweety birds flying around and waking up here."

He recounted the money and stuffed it into his jean pocket—being sure it was the pocket and not a hole in his pants.

"Anything going tomorrow? I think I got one more fight

left in this body."

"The fans love you, Steve 'The Rubberband Man' Cerroni." The boss snickered, and his eyes glistened as he imagined the marquee lit up with the name. "Hard not to when you fight almost every weekend. Tell you what, come back in two days and we'll put you in with this new stud I found. He's good, real good, and never been cut neither. It'll be a passing-of-the-torch match, if you will."

"Whatever you say, Mr. Goldman. As long as it pays the usual rate."

Cerroni's knuckles turned white as he gripped the arms of the chair and his arms shook as he strained to lift himself out of it. After a deep sigh of relief, he held out his hand to seal the deal. It was big tough hand. The skin was cracked and almost always bleeding. His fingernails were a permanent black and blue and scars were etched into the knuckles that made his hand look like bark on a tree.

Mr. Goldman's dainty hand shook Cerroni's quickly and he immediately pulled out a monogrammed handkerchief from his chest pocket and scrubbed the blood away, trying to hold back a grimacing look of disgust.

It was nothing Cerroni wasn't used to. At this point he would be more worried if he didn't hear people talk behind his back about his looks. The years of abuse radiated from the fighter. Every wheeze and moan and ache and bruise had become normal to the grizzled veteran. His jaw hurt when he chewed, and his head spun when he closed his eyes. He could hardly remember a time when he felt healthy or gave a wound the proper time to heal. But he had a reputation to uphold. The Rubberband Man must bounce back.

Cerroni left the office and limped his way to the locker room carrying a grin. He knocked on each brick of the cinder block wall at eye level, the same way he would every time he walked down the dimly lit corridor, feeling its cool and icy touch while listening intently to the lonely echo of his footsteps and the slight hum of a dull single light bulb.

He quickly packed his things and walked out of the locker room door at the end of the hall. It slammed shut behind him as he walked out of the arena and into the alleyway with his duffel bag in tow. The comforting smell of sweaty socks and the gym was left behind and now he faced the grimy streets, which glistened with a fresh coating of rain that sprinkled from the gloomy night sky and he smelled the vile odor of severely rotted trash long forgotten, or ignored, by the trash crews—much like the rest of the neighborhood he was strolling through.

Cerroni carried on through the worsening rain, his boots squishing with each step as water cozied its way into the insole of his worn shoes. Up and down the street the various street vendors stopped stocking their carts and sweeping the sidewalk to look upon this beaten-down man with childlike wonder.

"Steve, Steve, here take this," many of them said as he gave them a moment of his time.

Before Cerroni knew it, he was being dragged down with paper bags full of food and supplies. They patted him on the back and thanked him for another entertaining fight and tried to coach him, as all experts from the comfort of the recliner tended to do, on how to win next time. As much as he loved the longtime residents, he didn't like sitting outside with a pocket full of cash and took the advice quickly and with a nervous smile and continued in stride.

Suddenly, the streetlights stopped working and Cerroni knew he was near home. Trash littered the streets and the homeless took solace from the steamy heat erupting out of the manhole covers.

The entrance to his apartment did not look inviting at all. It was dilapidated and chunks of the stoop were missing. In fact, one would think the building was abandoned if not for the occasional light flickering through the dirty windows scaling up the building's wall.

The entry gate opened with a rusty rattle, nearly falling off its one good hinge, and dragged across the cement floor with a frightening cry. Cerroni quickly made his way to his flat down the hall. The locks sprung open and he jerked the tricky door before gently closing it shut behind him.

He dropped the bags on the rickety kitchen table and opened the fridge to find a few cans of beer and a loaf of Italian bread.

He ripped off a generous chunk of bread, cracked opened the beer and took a long, refreshing sip. He stood there for a while and did not move and he did not think. He just drank. Before he knew it, the beer was empty and that shocked him back into reality.

He then moved his way to the pantry and reached his way deep into the cabinet and felt around until his hand hit an old tin coffee can. On it was a masking tape label that read: *For my boy.*

Cerroni wrestled into his jean pocket, pulled out his earnings and shoved it all into the can. In a drawer he found a crumbled-up piece of paper and tried to flatten it out on the counter. It was covered in numeric scribbles. He looked down at the bottommost number and did some mental math, figuring there was now fifteen thousand dollars in the jar with the newest addition. Once satisfied with the math he promptly crumbled up the paper and threw it back in the drawer and shoved the jar back into the far reaches of the pantry cabinet.

With a new beer in hand he sat down on a busted-up recliner found on the curb and turned on the TV. But his attention was held elsewhere and he grabbed at a picture on the side table. It used to be a lovely family picture of a mother and her child, but the face of the mother was ripped away. All that remained, and mattered to Cerroni, was the gleeful smile of his six-year-old boy that warmed his aching soul and made a tear fall down his cheek and gave him enough peace to doze off for the rest of the night.

By the time Cerroni came back to the arena two days later, his face was as normal as it could be. He was still an ugly black and blue but swelling under his eyes went down enough for him to see and his nose was straightened enough so he could breathe, at least a little bit. He began to stretch and shadowbox before getting his hands taped and dressed in his boxing trunks. Soon enough Mr. Goldman came into the room and gave a wide-mouth smile.

"Ah, my boy. I'm glad you showed up. The place is jam-packed for your last fight."

"I'm just happy you kept paying me to come back," Cerroni chuckled. "But Mr. Goldman, I'd like to thank you for taking care of me all these years. I don't know if Maria will let me see my boy but at least he will have some walking around money when he gets older."

"You'll always have a place here, Steve. I'm a family

man, you know. And with the crowds you have brought in over the years . . . well, let's just say you're like family . . . and so is that boy—if he is what keeps you coming back. Find me after the show and we will see if we can find something a little less dangerous for you to do."

The cheers of the crowd flooded inside the locker room as Mr. Goldman opened the door to the arena floor. The chants of "Cerr-oni, Cerr-oni" filled his head and he shoved his hands into his trademark golden gloves. The leather clashed together as he punched his hands. His trainer draped his black robe with gold trim on him and Cerroni jogged his way to the ring where the young, up-and-coming star stood waiting.

In the middle of the ring he met his opponent for the first time. He towered over Cerroni. Keith Johnson appeared to be chiseled out of marble. His body was free from any scars, bruises, or fat. Cerroni held out his gloves and looked Johnson squarely in the eye.

"You ready, kid?"

Johnson scoffed, touched his gloves, and turned back into the corner while giving out a bellowing laugh.

"This guy looks worse than a punching bag, I won't even break a sweat."

Cerroni chuckled and gave a nod to the ref.

"Hey, Mick, how's the kids?"

"They're good, Stevie. Have a good fight, alright?"

The bell rung and Cerroni and Johnson danced around the ring.

Johnson glided on the tips of his toes, while Cerroni clunked around. He held his arms up high and held his head low, watching the eyes of Johnson. Johnson jabbed and caught Cerroni square in the jaw and jolted back as Cerroni countered with a hook that missed by a few feet.

"Come, on. This isn't even fair. He's too slow to hit a dead body."

Cerroni caught his breath and dove into Johnson, ducking his head and throwing a left-handed punch towards Johnson's ribs. He spun out of the way and hit Cerroni with a quick uppercut.

Cerroni's head began to spin and his ears rang with a high-pitched hiss and his eyes burned as he tried to find his balance. Johnson sprung on the attack. He hit him with multiple combos and quick jabs, smashing his ribs and breaking his nose.

Cerroni turtled. He cried out in pain and blood shot out his mouth and it started to run down his nose. Only the saving grace of the bell singling the end of Round One protected him. He spit what blood was left in his mouth and began to crack up laughing as he fell down onto the stool.

Johnson looked at him confused and almost frightened.

"This guy's insane," he told his corner. "It's like he wants an ass kicking."

"They don't call him the 'Rubberband Man' for nothing," his coach responded.

The bell rang for Round Two and Cerroni pounced, attempting to take Johnson off guard. He went back in for the same attack. Ducking his head and throwing a punch to Johnson's ribs. However, Cerroni guessed Johnson would counter and he backed off. Dodging the uppercut, Cerroni threw a hook with his right hand into Johnson's exposed side.

Johnson stumbled as the punch connected and felt his

lungs shutter as the wind was knocked out of him.

Cerroni punched again and again and finished his move with a strong hook to Johnson's face.

"Put your hands up and get out of there," Johnson's corner screamed.

Johnson listened and escaped as Cerroni gave chase. Cerroni chuckled and shuffled his way to cut his opponent off. He watched him cautiously, expecting retaliation and rose his hands high above his head. Johnson moved in and searched for a hole. The two exchanged blows back and forth, Johnson connecting far more often than Cerroni—who was now a bloody mess.

The second-round bell rang out and the crowd erupted in cheers. The next few rounds were dominated by Johnson and Cerroni hardly got in a punch.

"He won't go down. What is he made of?" Johnson said at the end of Round Nine.

"Don't worry about that, just finish the last round strong," the coach pleaded. "You've already won this. Don't take any risks."

The bell signaling the last round rang and Cerroni gave a quick raise of his fist to the crowd and the arena rumbled like an earthquake from the fans who cried out their support. He took a deep breath and charged at Johnson, who was hardly ready. He ducked and weaved and threw punches that Johnson couldn't keep up with. Cerroni broke his charge and caught his breath again. Johnson was hurt. He glided around the ring and tried to hide his pain. With one minute to go Cerroni went back on the attack. He threw two quick jabs to the face and started a hook to the body. When Johnson dropped his hands to block the hook Cerroni grinned.

"Gotcha."

Cerroni changed course and threw a shattering punch square into Johnson's face that hit like a bomb. Johnson stumbled and fell into the ropes and tumbled to the ground. Cerroni, panting, tried to regain his composure but couldn't help but show off a big, childlike smile to the crowd. Johnson looked around in a dream state but his eyes quickly caught sight of the specks of blood falling from his face and staining the once-white mat.

The crowd was silent. Johnson had never bled or been knocked down before. Many fans were surprised his blood was red like everyone else's. Johnson sprang to his feet and was fuming. He jolted towards Cerroni in a blind rage and treated him like a punching bag.

The ten-second warning knocks called out and Johnson pushed harder and faster. Cerroni couldn't keep up and was trying to block punches that were thrown seconds before. The ref jumped in as soon as the bell rang and Cerroni fell to the floor like a rag doll.

He heard the crowd cheering his name, even in defeat, and could see them rising to their feet for a standing ovation. Lying limp on the mat he smiled, coughing up blood.

He rose his shaky arm up high and acknowledged the fans and spit his mouthguard onto the mat.

"For my boy," he muscled out before blacking out.

Just in time

The cool fall air pierced through Will's face mask while he sat patiently between two trees, remaining completely motionless as he stared into the distance. He let out a deep breath and in the corner of his eye noticed the steamy fog rise and quickly dissipate. It made him smile and he knew it was another fine morning for a hunt, just like every morning spent in the field is.

A group of black specks rustled the tall grass in front of him, about a hundred yards out, and Will slowly rose his binoculars to his eyes. Three toms and two hens were strutting, seemingly without rhyme or reason towards the woods. The toms moved with a certain confidence, much like a king walking through a kingdom. They held their heads high, beaks to the sky, looking over their land. The hens pecked at the ground and scavenged for food, following the flock as they moved about, never straying too far from the toms. Without fear or worry they moved towards the tree line, unsuspecting of the threat sitting deep in the woods dressed in camo garb. With grace he moved the gun to the tree beside him and pulled a slate call out of his bag.

With quick, jerking motions he scratched the wooden stick onto the stone surface. The call, which replicated the sounds of a turkey, broke the silence of the peaceful morning and he abruptly stopped and stared back through his binoculars. One of the toms stopped and rose its neck higher and higher and quickly looked around for the strange call. Soon after he shook it off and went back to grazing.

Will scratched down on the slate again. This time with longer and harder yelps, followed by short cackles in attempts to regain the tom's attention. The tom took notice and puffed up. It nearly doubled in size and its tail feathers expanded into a beautiful fan.

Behind the mask Will was smiling from ear to ear. It was a big turkey. The kind of turkey to make all the chilly mornings and stiff backs from hours of sitting on the ground worth it. It had been a hard season. He saw plenty of turkey but the years of hunting had made him picky and wise. No longer was he out for the thrill of the kill and just getting as much game as he was allowed.

Will realized his part in nature. For thousands of years humans thought they were above the ecosystem, better than the other animals and detached from the circle of life, but Will learned otherwise. Each year he came closer and closer to the conclusion that it is only the brain that set humans apart. Although a mighty advantage, it is also mankind's downfall. Somewhere along the line humans forgot they were part of the natural world. They created a new world on top of the old and turned their backs on what once was. New homes were created out of artificial materials and neighborhoods were carved into quaint spots in the world and surrounded by convenience that further cut up the Earth. Will took this to heart and cursed his kind. He watched the old world falter. The animals grew weaker while the populations continued to climb and the food and cover they desperately needed was only getting smaller and smaller. Now he tried to do his part as a being in the ecosystem with advanced intelligence. He hunted for conservation and not to just protect the land, but to sustain it and ultimately make it thrive again.

Will rested his head on the tree supporting him and got lost in his thoughts and dreams of a more natural world. Soon the approaching footsteps and cackles of the turkey brought him back to reality and like a general during a war he theorized the best plan of attack on the fly. He asked himself if it would be smarter to stay put and bring them into the woods, or should he crawl out into the field? He weighed the risk and rewards of each and decided to meet them halfway. After all, he thought, the only thing you can rely on is yourself and if you want something done do it.

Will took off his backpack and took the only two things he needed to complete the task—his shotgun and the slate call. The pump gun was a well-worn 12-gauge he had had since he was a boy. Back then it was clumsy in hand, but true experience offers real change and now it sat comfortably, like an extension of himself. The gun was like one of his closest friends, in a sense. The kind of friend where there is no dignity or shame to hide behind and conversation comes as easily as talking to yourself.

He opened the action, just a sliver, on the old gun and made sure a shell was inside. After that he scratched on the call, stood still for a couple of long seconds, and headed out. Will stayed crouching, zigzagging from tree to tree. At every other tree he peered out at the turkeys and went back on the call, keeping them interested in the mysterious caller. When he was about twenty feet from the tree line he fell to his belly and crawled as slowly as he could to a tree just inside the line.

The tom Will had his eye on continued to puff up and keep his beak held high, glancing around for the sight of his new rival. The hens became shifty and tried to move closer and closer to the woods. The tom seemingly was getting angry and started to hop up and down, bringing up the dirt and making a cloud of dust around the flock. Will, now at the tree, moved as quietly as possible to get into a crouched shooting position. He anchored his body on the trunk and slowly raised the stock to his cheek and had his eye following the length of the barrel and aimed at the head of the turkey.

He couldn't believe how big the bird was now that he was within shooting range. Its long beard swayed magnificently in the breeze as it strutted and its tail feathers towered over its back. They were beaten and ruffled and it was clear now this king of the field was old. It was the exact kind of animal Will wanted.

Adrenaline flowed through Will as he watched it continue to thrash and move about, challenging the unknown call to a fight but he kept his aim true. The bead of the gun stayed on target and he sat there, for what felt like hours, waiting for the tom to calm himself and relax its feathers, giving him a clean and steady shot to preserve the meat. His arms began to grow tired, but he knew any sudden movement now would cause the creature to fly off. A turkey didn't grow this old without dodging his fair share of hunters. Just when he thought he had enough the hens began to move in the opposite direction and the tom relaxed itself. No new calls had been coming and the threat of another turkey to his flock was seemingly gone.

Will clicked off the safety and gave a loud whistle. The tom became startled and extended his neck and peered into the forest. Will fired his shot. It echoed through the forest and out into the field. The other turkeys sprinted away, flapping their wings to get away. Will's tom instantly fell to the ground, with a few feathers slowly falling back to earth after it.

He ripped down his face mask and gave out an exhilarating breath that filled the cool fall air and wiped off the almost-frozen sweat from his forehead. He looked up, thanking God, and jumped out of the tree brush and looked down at his kill.

The fanned-out tail made Will's eyes wide as he inspected it and he imagined it hanging on the mantle—a constant reminder of the hunt and the great game he encountered. He then placed his hand on the dead bird and paid his respects to the animal and thanked it for the life it lived, the life it gave, and the food it would provide him and his family. He then lifted the heavy bird up and looked at the long spurs on its feet that were starting to curve and judged it to be close to four years old. He then slung it on his back and felt its heavy weight on his shoulders and began the long walk back home where his family would be waiting to prepare for the holiday season.

Lessons learned

It was three hours till dawn and his son was still asleep in the bed. Will raised his big rough hands and scratched the beard he grew out each fall. He looked down at his feet surround by bag after bag of hunting supplies, decoys, and clothing and gave out a sigh.

Jameson, a chocolate lab, jumped over a duffel bag and sat at Will's feet. He bent down and scratched behind the big dog's ear and gently said, "Go get him, boy." Jameson's ears pricked with excitement and he jumped back over the gear and made a sprint to the boy's room. I'm beginning to think the dog is more excited than the boy, he thought.

Will went out for some fresh air as he waited for his son to get up. The quietness of the dark before a hunt reminded him of an old friend. The kind of friend where no matter how much time has passed nothing has changed and conversation and laughter happen in an instant. The cool misty air around the cabin filled his lungs and he exhaled a deep cool breath. Suddenly, the stillness was interrupted by the scream of Colin.

"Ah, Jameson, what are you doing? It is too early to play," the nine-year-old rang out.

"But not too early to load the truck," Will called out.

Will made his way back inside the cabin, the wood floor creaked as he stepped. He went to his spot, like every father has, and sat down in an old leather chair and hung his head back while he waited for Colin to put the endless amount of gear in the truck.

"Are we really going to need all of this, dad?"

"Probably not," he chuckled. "But you always want to have more than you need, just in case."

"But it really is a pain."

"Oh, I know. That is why I had a son and why you're doing all the hard work," he said with an obnoxious smile on his face.

Colin squinted his eyes angrily at his dad as he dragged the last duffel bag, about twice the size of the boy, full of decoys, out to the car. Will got up excitedly and with a happy-go-lucky strut went to the guns safe and looked over all of his guns before settling on his trusty 12-gauge.

"You're so embarrassing," Colin said as he walked out of the cabin in disgust.

Will looked into his rearview mirror to see his son staring out the window, struggling to see what was out in the distance and Jameson, faithful as always, was laying his head on the boy's lap trying to help.

"Don't worry, in a couple hours that is when the magic happens."

"What magic?" Colin asked.

"When the sun rises and everything wakes up. Knowing you and how you like to sleep, this is probably the first time you've beat the sunup."

"Not true, I stay up all night a lot. You just don't know because I'm sneaky and I'll play games while you sleep and you don't even know."

Will tried to get angry, but it was no use. He did the same things, like laying under the bed with a book and a flashlight and fake sleeping when footsteps came by the door. It was a rite of passage for a kid.

It wasn't a long drive to camp but Colin was getting antsy. He continued to stare into the dark, hoping to catch a sight of this so-called magic but he saw nothing of the sort. The only thing he did find was a certain kind of boredom. The kind that made him feel like he was confined to a jail cell and unable to move. Eventually the night sky broke his spirit and he cried out.

"Dad, are we there yet? I wanna go hunting. We are going to miss all the ducks."

"Patience, boy, there is a lot of work to do before we go to the blind. We must set up camp first and foremost. The ducks aren't going anywhere."

"But what if we don't see any, what if they are gone and we wasted our time?"

"That is possible. We may not even hear a quack. But remember this: there is a lot more to hunting then shooting game. A time wasted hunting is not time wasted at all. You'll figure it out soon, I promise."

At the camp, Will put up their tent in between two large trees. The ping of the hammer butt hitting the stakes pierced through the silence. He threw the sleeping bags and bag of clothes in the tent and closed it tight and hammered a few nails in the tree to hang up their packs and wet clothes later.

The sun was starting to rise and the light started to sneak past the trees and just like that Colin knew what his dad meant. In an instant everything went from quiet and dark to loud and bright. He looked around and thought he traveled a million miles. All the scenery changed. The birds chirped their morning songs and he could hear squirrels scurrying down the trees and rustling on the forest floor. To the left of the tent there was a bank of the river. He swore it just then started to flow and rumble now that he saw it with his own eyes.

"Where . . . where did this all come from?"

"I told you the sunrise is magic."

The two put their waders on and put a camo life jacket on Jameson and Will loaded up his pockets with shells. Colin was still too young to handle a gun, but Will thought it was the right time to show him the ropes and bring him out. It was the father-son bonding time he had been looking forward to since Colin was a baby.

The two had always gotten along and they loved each other very much, but Will always felt guilty that there was this part of him he couldn't show Colin yet. He wanted to take him out and show him the borderless land of nature and the experience that has had a grip on humans since the dawn of time.

Will called Jameson over and he came to a heel and looked up at his master with ever-loving eyes and tail vigorously wagging in the dirt. Will bowed his head and waved Colin over. Colin looked confused. The family had their strong faith, but they had never been a strict religious family and never openly prayed together or went to church.

Will then pulled out a long silver chain and prayed for a successful and honest hunt. Will started to put it around his neck like he had so many times before. Today, he stopped. He kneeled down and put the chain around his son's neck.

"This is my lucky charm. I wear it each time I shoot and hunt. In honor of your first time in the field today, I want you to wear it."

On the chain was a silver medallion of St. Hubert (the patron saint of hunters) and the brass from the shot shell that killed his first bird.

"It is important for me to keep this," he said, fumbling with the brass in his fingers. "I took that animal's life and I wanted to keep that memory with me out of respect for the animal. We hunters take pride in honing our skills and being able to take down game cleanly and only what our limits allow. We respect nature and we respect the animals in nature, even in their deaths. We use the meat we harvest to feed our loved ones and we thank God for allowing us to harvest the game as humanly as possible. Colin, you need to understand that if you want to be not just a good hunter, but also a good person."

"Yes, sir," he said. He couldn't take his eyes off the brass and held onto it tightly.

Will smiled and they headed towards the blind. Jameson could barely contain himself. He jumped up and down and strutted proudly on Will's left and Colin, on the right, watched his dad look cooler than ever with his gun rested atop his shoulder and his camo boonie hat—that until now he thought was lame—pulled over his eyes. The three of them walked calmly in a line but it was obvious that the three of them wanted to break out in a mad dash.

The three of them sat in the custom-built blind that Will designed after a baseball dugout. There was an overhanging roof that slanted backwards, allowing rainwater to not impair their vision. The front was, for the most part, wide open aside from the tree branches and cattails put around it for cover and a single wooden bar that served as a footrest, if needed. There were no cushioned seats in the blind, just wooden benches. However, Will always packed two folded cushions with back support and a rubber dog bed. At the two ends of the blind were two doggy doors, giving Jameson two exits to the pond ahead of them.

"There is one more thing, Colin."

"Yes, Dad?"

"I'm going to need you to take this and call in the ducks," Will said, smiling.

Colin couldn't believe it. He was scared to take the duck call out of his dad's hand. He was sure this was another one of his dad's famous tricks. He was certain he would pull it away at the last second.

"I'm serious, boy. Take it before the ducks come."

It was a simple tool but it alone could be the difference between pass and fail. Colin took one more long look before grabbing it and examined the call further. Like a knight and his sword he held it proudly and firmly grasped it out in front of him. Colin spent a lot of time watching videos how to use one and on occasion, without his dad's knowledge, would borrow a call and try to use it.

In a matter of moments a small flock of ducks could be heard and soon thereafter seen in the distance. Will slapped Colin on the arm again and again to get his son's attention and didn't stop until Colin almost screamed.

"Go on, call em' in. Come on. Come on."

Colin got ready. He wrapped his hand around the bottom of the call and wrapped his lips around the top. He breathed in deeply and blew like he was playing a solo at a jazz concert. Jameson pricked his ears and got bug-eyed watching Colin and Will burst out laughing. He wiped a tear from his eyes and took the call from Colin.

"You know when Mom starts yelling at us and we just go outside and ignore her? That is exactly what you just did to those ducks . . . nagged them to death."

Will showed him some better techniques and gave Colin back the call and let him practice. Will nodded his head with approval. They were in luck and another flock of mallards flew in their direction and Will gave his son the cue to start calling. Quiet quacks came from Colin and gradually got louder and louder. Then he mixed up his calls, going from his basic quacks to a greeting call and some feeding calls.

Will was amazed by how well he was picking it up. Colin kept on calling, eyes glued to the sky and Will pushed off his safety and raised his gun. The four mallards flew by and started to descend into the pond where a gaggle of decoys Will set up rested. *Boom, boom,* the shots echoed out around them with a deafening cry. Will racked open the gun and the final spent shell flew out in a cloud of gunpowder.

"Dead duck, fetch," he bellowed.

Jameson ran through his doggy door, jumped and hit the water with a splash and paddled his way out to the furthest dead duck. Colin jumped out of his seat and watched the dog work and, to Colin's amazement, find the real duck in a pool of plastic ones.

"Isn't that something?"

"Right there is my favorite part of the hunt. I love watching the dog do his thing."

Jameson, with a big drake mallard in his mouth, walked back through the doggy door and dropped the bird at Will's feet.

"Good boy, go fetch." Will pointed back out the water. Jameson followed his point and caught onto the scent of the dead duck and jumped back in to find the second bird.

Just as before, he found it and brought it back and dropped the bird at Will's feet and he was praised generously before the inevitable happened. Jameson shook his fur dry. Will laughed as the water sprayed his face and he saw Colin push his hands in front of him to stop the onslaught of water.

"Let's check out our winnings," Will said.

Will raised the two mallards in his hands, they had a nice weight to them and looked beautiful. He handed one over to Collin who took it nervously.

"Are you sure it's dead?"

"Haha, I'm sure. You did real good calling them in. You are a natural," Will said proudly. "Couldn't ask for a better hunting partner."

Collin turned away blushing. "So what do we do now?"

"Well we can stay a bit longer and see what else we can get, we are allowed a few more birds."

Back at camp the evening was beginning to set in and the three of them broke for dinner. Jameson was muzzle deep in his food bowl, eating a well-deserved meal and Will turned on his camp stove to make blueberry pancakes and sausage.

"After we eat we will take a duck and you'll clean them to cook for a late night snack. The rest we have to save for Mom."

Collin's face turned a sickly white and he lost his appetite. "But . . . but . . . I don't know how to clean them."

"If you're gonna come out hunting, you sure as hell are going to learn," Will stated. "Ducks are easy, just wait till you get a deer."

After a quick lunch, Will sat on the riverbed and enjoyed the pleasantness outdoors. Collin played with Jameson and kicked around a soccer ball. After a while Will found himself in a chair, enjoying a glass of whiskey and Coke. This is the life, he thought, and he nodded off for a quick nap.

Seeing his dad asleep, Collin reached into his pocket and pulled out an empty shot shell from the morning. He made sure he grabbed the first one that ejected from the gun and he quickly stuck it in his pocket without his dad seeing. He examined it longingly and held onto it tightly in his hands and began to wonder how he could make this into his very own necklace.

To be somebody

Sitting at the Albert Dock has always been my favorite pastime. Here I can people-watch as they walk into the restaurants and bars. It's funny, they don't even realize the history they are walking into, but people never realize anything anymore. Hunched over the railing I look into the dark water and glare at a familiar face. It's old and worn, with my wrinkles covered by a thick unkempt beard, and long shaggy hair. It's all a sad attempt to hide my true age.

I've always liked looking into my eyes though, it sure beat looking into my ex-wives'. These eyes, these eyes have seen a lot, but have done so little. I guess you could say I'm a coward. I was always afraid to try in school, sports, and even just talking to real people. If a ball came at me, I'd run away. If I was given a test, I would have an anxiety attack. I am the city bum after all, and I barely do that right. I can't beg for cash, I'm too scared to ask and start to shake. The cardboard sign I made can't keep still long enough for people to even read.

So, I just watch, hoping someone notices me, but they don't. That's me, a run-of-the-mill coward. As the sun goes down, I venture to Mathew Street and talk to my old buddy, Statue John. He doesn't talk much, of course, but he is a good listener. I tell him if I could only do it again, it would be different. I'd be somebody. I'd be the one being watched. It's a good thought at least and I fall asleep in the road with the cool stone touching my skin as I wait for another day to end.

I feel a sharp pain in my side and wake in a coughing fit. I look down and see the expensive boot that just kicked me. I follow it up and it is attached to a sharp-dressed man. His black hair is slicked back, his boots polished and shining like the sun, and his jet-black suit fit him perfectly to the last stitch. I look at him and he to me and I can't quite get a read on him. The man looks trustworthy enough, but there is something about him that makes me feel weird.

"Can I help you, mate?" I stutter as my anxiety kicks in. He looks at me, with his eyes staring into my soul, and he stands there without making a sound and keeps me on pins and needles before responding. He reaches into his breast pocket and I am certain this is the end. But instead of the gun I am sure he has, he pulls out a golden case of cigarettes and puts one into his mouth.

"I think we can help each other. You see I'm Luke and I hear you want another chance?"

His voice is out of this time. He has an American accent, a '40s transatlantic accent, like the kind you used to be able hear on old-timey radio.

"What are you gettin' at? How you even know what I want? What, were you spying on me when I was talking to Statue John?"

He lights his cigarette and takes a long hit and gives me a smile. He responds, but not before blowing a thick cloud of smoke into my face. Its toxic aroma fills my nose. The smell of tobacco makes me dizzy and I feel like I'm falling through a factory's smokestack. "Listen here, I can make you a somebody. It won't be this year but I'll treat you right—you just have to do something for me." I've never been one for gambling but something about this man makes me want to do things for him. Yes, I would give it all to be somebody, I tell him. His smile grows wider and wider and he blows one more puff of smoke. This smoke has a different aroma. It smells fresh like a spring morning and it is mysterious and takes me over like a spell. My feet stumble, my knees buckle, and I hit the ground with a *thud*, but I feel no pain. The last thing I remember is Luke walking into the shadows with smoke rising from his mouth and him letting out a wicked laugh. I try to see where he went, but my eyes are getting heavy and they close before my head hits the ground.

Hey! Wake up, you're on! My eyes flash open, head pounding, heart racing. "Where . . . who . . . Statue John?"

"I don't know what this statue business is about, but John is my name, John Lennon. Get on the stage mate, you're up."

"John Lennon, you can't be, you're . . . de . . . de . . ." For some reason I can't spit out the word. He yells at me some more and sends me onto the stage. There are others on the stage; they greet me like we are best friends, but I have never seen them before. They are dressed in button-down shirts and skinny ties and their hair is combed over with pounds of grease. It looks like they have been shopping at a thrift shop. I have a guitar strapped to me, which is odd since I don't know how to play any instrument, let alone a guitar. I want to stop moving but my feet keep going towards the stage until I'm under the hot stage lamp. I can feel the sweat start to build on my brow, but I feel calm.

The drum beats, and the singer starts singing, and next thing I know I'm strumming the guitar like I've been playing my whole life. The next thirty minutes go by in a daze and I keep looking at hands playing the instrument. It is like someone is controlling me like a marionette puppet. I look away from myself and out at the crowd cheering us on after our final song. Hundreds of girls are screaming, guys are applauding, and I can just make out one man near the back, in a jet-black suit, walking away with a puff of smoke coming from his mouth.

I must get to him. I try to run after him, but I'm stopped by an energetic little man yelling "We did it, we got signed!" I'm surrounded by my apparent bandmates and they guide me into a back room. I sit down and jump right back up. I'm looking into the mirror but the man looking back is not the me I'm used to. But here I am. I move my arms and the reflection moves back. I turn my head and pull at my hair and it again follows suit. My shaggy hair is cut down like a proper schoolboy and my old and worn skin is youthful and beardless like a child. The only way I am absolutely sure it is me is my eyes. I start for the door but I'm stopped by the short man again. He starts listing off things to do and his excitement can't be contained but I push myself past him. I must find him, I must find Luke.

I weave in between empty guitar cases and amps and work my way from backstage and into the main ballroom and step onto the middle of the floor and my legs stop and I feel a chill run down my back. I'm in the Cavern Club. I just played in the Cavern Club. I couldn't believe it. It was hard to see from the blinding stage lights when I was playing, but now it is clear as day. The famous brick arches of a cellar-turned-nightclub are all around me and if I need more convincing, I turn around to look at the stage. My jaw drops. Right behind me, where I was just playing, is the famous brick backdrop wall covered in bright neon paint with some of the most well-known Liverpool band names. I must be dreaming. But I couldn't enjoy the moment much longer. It is more important to find Luke and see what is going on here.

I charge up the stairs to get to the surface. The night lights blind me and I come to a screeching halt. When my eyes focus, I look around, searching for him. He couldn't have gotten too far. I look up and down the road and start to take off in a sprint but there he is in plain sight, just leaning against the wall waiting with a smoke in his hand.

"Looking for someone?"

I grab his lapel and pull him close to me and yell, "What the hell is going on?"

"Exactly what you wanted—to be somebody. Don't tell me you already forgot, Jack? You said you'd give it all and I gave you what you asked for. Don't you realize? Look around, this is the town you know, just 1961 not 2013. But now it's time to repay me to keep up this little charade."

He gives me that menacing smile again and I know I am in trouble. I let him go and he opens his mouth. "What I need from you is to take out a little order on a, uh, big time guy . . . if you get my drift. You may know him, his name is Elvis, and he is another guy who wanted to be someone. But you see, he didn't want to uphold his bargain."

He told me I'd get on a plane to the USA, play a few shows and take him out, or I wouldn't be a somebody anymore. The mini-USA tour was great. We played shows almost every night and each night the crowds got bigger and bigger and I felt untouchable. The girls drooled over me and the boys wished they could be me. I finally knew what it was like to be a star. Eventually our tour bus drove into Tennessee and we took a little detour, just as Luke predicted.

Memphis is a nice place, a rock and roll city like Liverpool. The only difference is someone's blood would be spilled on Memphis soil and it is all because of me. I sit in my hotel and think about all the things that would happen and have happened in just a few short weeks. It is impossible. It must be a dream, but here I am, and I can't wake up, so it must be real.

I look over to my right and there's a gun sitting on the hotel night table. I'm not sure how it got there, but it suddenly showed up. It's brand new, and I could look at myself in its bright shiny chrome. Next to it is one golden bullet. I pick up the gun and hold it in my hand and feel its weight. The cold handle warms in my hand as I tighten my grip around the handle. I point it at the unfamiliar face in the mirror and pull the trigger. Click. Too easy, it's too easy to kill. Just one little slip of the finger is all I need. I'm to meet Elvis in twenty minutes.

Graceland is exactly how I imagined it. A little slice of heaven and not one blade of grass out of place. It's a big house and has expensive cars, you know the whole shebang. Elvis greets me with open arms and offers me tea since "that's how you Brits like it." I can't stay too long, I tell him. Truthfully, I have all the time in the world, but I just don't want to hear the life story of someone I have to kill. We talk a bit and he asks me about myself. I tell him a few things, made up things, and finish my tea. Then I take one last look at him. Here I am sitting in front of Elvis and he actually cares what I have to say and all I can really muster to say is "I don't have much to say, I hardly know, this new me."

The fear takes over and I know what must be done. I was feeling happy for the first time in a long time and I didn't want it to change. So I pull the gun out of my jacket and point it right between Elvis's eyes and he falls to his knees and begs me not to do it. I tell him, "Luke doesn't like a bad deal." My arm is shaking and I can't steady the gun. He pleads to me for his life and promises to make things right with Luke if he can just have more time. He tells me about his family and his real hopes and dreams. Not just being famous but the things that matter. The real legacy he wants to leave behind.

I start to second-guess myself and I close my eyes and think. Why do I need to do this, is being somebody worth it? Sure, I'm not always the happiest and I made a lot of mistakes, but that's on me. It was my choices that got me to where I am at and I can't take shortcuts to the promised land. At the end of it all I want to enjoy what I've done for myself.

As the gun falls to my side a thunderous boom shakes the home and there is Luke, only this time he is not smiling. Anger takes over as he yells. It is so loud I fall to the floor like a bomb went off. Luke seems to grow taller and taller the louder he yells. The lights shatter and Elvis passes out from fright. "Do you know who I am? Nobody breaks my deals, do you hear!"

In tears I respond, "You made me a somebody, but I don't want it this way. I don't want to be controlled. I already am a somebody. I am me."

The shaking stops and Luke had that ever-menacing smile on his face. "You think *I* would make you a famous musician just like that? Ha. You mustn't know who I am, boy. You would have been somebody alright. You would be the man who killed Elvis!" My heart stops, my world is shaken. I don't know how to respond. I am speechless and can only sit in the tears streaming down my face. I was played for a fool by the devil himself and just for his amusement. The words "you have disappointed me" echo in the room and smoke fills my lungs once more and I hit the ground hard, only to wake up instantly in what seemed like the modern Liverpool I had come to know.

I ran to the nearest street vendor. My head is pounding and I grab the nearest newspaper and almost tear it in half to see today's date. 2013, the paper says. I throw the paper down and run until I am back at the Albert Dock. There are people walking into clubs and I barrel past them, shoving a few of them to the ground, but I have to get to the rail. I throw my head over and search my reflection in the water below and I cry out tears of joy when I see a familiar face at last. My old worn wrinkled skin glistens off the water and my beard and messy hair cover what wrinkles it can. I am back, the nightmare is over. Not many get to deal with the devil and live to tell about it, I think. My anxiety disappears and I feel like a new man. Maybe it wasn't a nightmare after all but a godforsaken, or should I say devil-forsaken, wake-up call. I let out a sigh of relief and sit down against the old brown stone wall and feel content for the first time in my life.

The last conversation

On their deathbeds, two men lay in an old-age home. The lives of these two old men have been intertwined since the days of old. Back to a time when their spirits were youthful and full of pride and passion. During a great war they fought against one another and as things had to be, one became the winner and the other the loser.

The winner was recognized for his valor and heralded a hero. Until it no longer fit, he wore his uniform and proudly donned his medals on his chest and afterwards he wouldn't be seen without slipping on his black hat that read *Veteran* in golden letters. In turn, the loser was ridiculed, cast to the shadows and hated. He was stripped of his honor. His uniform was burned, and medals he earned were melted and his name, unless he wished for public scrutiny, was changed so he could find a sliver of salvation in the post-war era.

On their final day the winner shuffled gingerly into the loser's room and he was greeted with a frail, but friendly, wave telling him to come closer. Long ago the fire in their bellies for fighting waned and it was decided the passion for war was best suited for the young and spirited. So now they gathered as confidants and friends. For only a hardened man could understand a hardened man.

"I'm afraid my time has all but run out, my dear friend," the winner said.

"I believe you are right, and I am soon to follow."

The two looked at each other longingly and held hands and decided to face death together and distracted themselves with conversation.

The loser admired the winner, as many had, and found a certain jealousy as he gazed upon him.

"You look so youthful, even as death's shadow begins to cast over you. Life must have been easy after the fighting. The parades, the free meals, and the smiles of children and the respect of their parents. But look at me. The war may have ended but the fighting never ended for me."

The winner looked at him with confusion and drew back his hand.

"On the outside it may seem as such, but inside is a constant storm. I'm haunted by the memories of battle and the screams of men fill my head and I can see each and every face whenever I close my eyes. I cannot sleep and I cannot be alone. The war never left me as it has never left you. But what I did was right and good and—"

The loser cut him off and mustered up enough strength to speak with a raised voice.

"Don't begin to give me that. That propaganda that was shoved down your throat. What makes you good, and I bad? Have you not committed the same crimes as I? Did you not murder, rape, and pillage? Is all blood that stains your hands from self-defense? That I doubt. Your words, your creed, don't set you apart. We are of the same cloth. Men sent to resolve the problems of bickering childlike adults who were too greedy to search for peace and understanding."

"It is true I have committed crimes. That I cannot deny. But I won't be judged on happenstance because I ended up on the winning side. I am but one man among hundreds of thousands."

The loser shook his head and let out an ugly breath. He rested his eyes on the winner and his old eyes sparked with a fire he thought he lost long ago.

"Yet for my happenstance and my random place of birth I was judged, ridiculed, and forced to change my identity just to survive. What you don't understand is you are no more a winner than I a loser. We were both played for fools, used for our youth and stripped of our innocence. You tell me you are haunted by the faces of the dead and the sounds of war. As am I. But you sit in front of me with pride and wear your hat and that helps cover your scars. Tell me, is it pride for surviving the horrors or for the attention and thanks it brings?"

The winner sat silently for a long while and began to weep.

"Yes, I have pride for my country. For winning. And I deserve thanks for sacrificing my youth in my old age. Damn me for being selfish. But my heart breaks for your struggle. I see your pain clearer now. Like me, you were just one man in a sea of faces and your actions did little, as did mine, to change the scales of war. It is true we were played for fools. Taught to obey and take direction without a second thought. But what would you have me do? The cards we have been dealt have all but been played.

"I just wish you to understand. I can't regret how my life has gone, not now. Not so close to the end. I just wish to know how it would have been if I were you. Even for a moment."

The winner wiped a final tear away and the conversation carried on a little longer, but he had his mind elsewhere and was busy concocting a plan. As he left the room and said goodnight, he told his onetime adversary, and now friend, thank you. It caught the loser off guard and he furrowed his brow.

The winner called out when he just left the door. "Hold on one more day, you old bag of bones."

In the common area the man waved to everyone to come near. The other residents walked over slowly, and the volunteers, nurses, and doctors came over with a nervous look of concern.

"I'm not sure if you ever knew, but the man in that room there," he pointed his cane in the direction, "is a veteran who fought in the same war as I but on the other side."

He looked around at the faces of shock by everyone and in a few he saw looks of anger set in.

He quickly continued.

"I need to ask you all a personal favor. There is no question he and I have but a few moments left in this world, so I beg of you all to visit him as soon as you can and thank him for his service or apologize for the way society has put him down."

The residents cursed and some turned away and others looked at him quizzically.

"But how can we do that, after all that happened?" a woman asked. "He is always such a grouch and never treats anyone but you nice and now you want us to thank him?"

"I know," the man said. "But he has opened my eyes this night. He is no different than me but for his luck and where he was born. He was called to service and followed his orders like a good soldier. But he has the misfortune of being haunted by the past and it continues even as we speak."

He continued his case and spoke the words the loser said and eventually the seed was planted and he hoped it would grow quickly. He watched the people's eyes and tried to overhear their conversations and what decisions they made. The winner soon felt comfortable going to bed and that his task would be completed.

The next morning a nurse came to the aid of the loser, as was her duty, and she went about her business as usual and took his vitals and fed him his breakfast and handed out his pills. But before she left, she sat on the foot of his bed and placed her hand on his knee and looked at him in a caring sort of way. He was confused but she continued to sit and eventually said, in a genuine way, thank you and I'm sorry.

He sat in a stunned silence and couldn't respond before she left. Throughout the day residents stuck their heads in and said hello and they all seemed to take an interest in his day and before any of them left they said thank you and he didn't know how to take it. Never had he garnered so much attention, he thought. Towards the end of the day the doctor came in for his usual rounds and the man asked him what had gotten into everyone. But the doctor played dumb and pretended he knew nothing and kept quiet on the matter and stuck to speaking only in medical terms. The man begged and pleaded to the doctor to have a heart. He told him he couldn't keep a secret to an old man and asked him, in the most serious tone he could, what had gotten into everyone.

The doctor looked up from his notes and over his glasses towards the man. He flipped the pages of his clipboard closed and stuck it under his arm and moved towards the man and looked him in the eyes.

"I guess we have all started to see things from a different perspective. So, thank you for that and everything else."

The loser laid back in his bed and watched the doctor leave the room. After hours of thinking it dawned him that his friend was up to his devilish games. His eyes swelled up and he fought back the tears. He achingly sat up and grabbed his walker and shuffled himself slowly down the hall to his friend's room. His door was closed and when he knocked there was no answer. The man knocked again and again. Like most soldiers he was a notoriously light sleeper, so he thought the knock would have easily woken him up. But still there was no answer.

He decided he couldn't wait and entered the winner's unlocked room. He was there lying in bed peacefully and the loser was a bit stunned.

"Well, didn't you hear me knocking there you big ol' dummy? I know what you did, putting up everyone in this darn home to treat me differently."

The man laid still in his bed and didn't respond.

"Well, what have you got to say for yourself?" he said. The old man shuffled his way next to the bed and gave the winner a shove.

The man in bed hardly moved and was ice cold. The gears in the loser's head started to turn and he burst into tears.

"No. Don't be dead, dammit. Not yet," he cried out. "Nurse, nurse, somebody."

The nurse heard the screams and rushed in. Accessing the scene, the nurse started the normal protocol when a resident left this world and brought in a volunteer to console the man and get him out of the way.

In the common area the man was in tears and it caused enough of a scene to get everyone to gather around and he began to talk to anyone that would listen.

"I didn't get a chance to tell him thanks. After all my moaning about it. He was the only person who ever understood what I felt. What it was like to be in the thick of it, even from the other side, and now he's gone, and I'll never be able to tell him."

The doctor from before came over and sat down next to the man and put his hand on his shoulder.

"I don't think you understand. He didn't want to be thanked. He had his moments, a whole lifetime of them, and now he wanted you to know you deserved it just as much. He was so sorry it took him so long to realize that."

Everyone in the home took a moment to mourn and sit with the old man. After a while he was getting tired and he went back to his own room and thought about the last conversation he had with his friend. His heart was broken and the man didn't know if he could go on. For the first time since the war, he got down on his knees and prayed and hoped somehow his old friend would get the message. He thanked him for understanding him and even after being on opposite sides, acknowledged him and befriended him and treated him like a human. He ended his night by telling the winner he better be warming the place up for him because he knew he would be on the way soon enough.

Father v. son
or an ongoing battle

Oyi! A deafening sound only a father makes rang out from the rocking chair in the front room.

Jacob, a ten-year-old boy, ran around the corner in a grimy pair of grass-stained overalls. His hands were covered in dirt and his hair was more like an unkempt ball of yarn.

"Yes, Dad?" he asked innocently.

"Care to explain why there is a trail of mud, about the size of a ten-year-old's shoe, all throughout the house and fingerprints all over *MY TV*?"

Jacob stood there, swaying about and looking around the room, not answering.

"Look at me when I'm talking to you." His dad's voice was starting to rise and losing patience.

Jacob looked further away from his dad's direction and closed his eyes tightly in defiance, like he was a clown entertaining at a birthday party.

The dad's hand slammed on the wooden table in front of him. An explosive shock rang through the house and you could hear Jacob's mom yelp a startled scream around the corner. The dad's face was turning red. He was thinking and began shaking from anger. Then he suddenly let out his anger in the form of a long puff of air and turned his furrowed brow and grinding teeth into a smile, but not a happy smile. It was the kind of smile that's made when you have outsmarted an opponent and you were about to defeat them without them knowing.

"I guess you're not in the mood for talking. Sounds like you won't mind spending some alone time in your room then."

The dad reached out his hand and demanded any electronics Jacob may have been hiding. He tried to pretend he had nothing on him, but the dad knew his game and took a frightening step closer to his son.

"Fine," Jacob snapped. Out of his pockets he drew out his Game Boy and cell phone and slammed them into his dad's outstretched hand.

Jacob snickered as he ran to his room. He thought he won. He didn't have to clean, didn't face a spanking, and got to be alone in his room. But he wasn't really alone, he told himself. There at his nearest convenience was a TV and a PlayStation and a computer.

He ran through the door of his room and like a stuntman, jumped up, and landed right in the middle of the bed. The controller to his PlayStation, sitting on the bed, flew up from the force of his landing and dropped right into his hands. The chime of the power button rang out, a heavenly sound to Jacob, and he smiled. Sucker, he thought to himself of his dad.

Jacob smiled and laughed out loud and then got serious.

"What game to play, what gayymeee tooo playyy?"

He looked up at his TV, ready to make an all-important decision but not before dread struck him and he felt the weight of the world fall onto his shoulders. Three words appeared on the TV. When put together they were the worst words in all the world. They made him feel sick to his stomach and he felt like he was being punched each time he read the dreaded words.

WI-FI NOT AVAILABLE

It danced around the screen gleefully. Tormenting him. Taunting him.

He screamed a painful "NOOOOOO" and then he heard the quiet laughter of his dad from the other side of the house.

"That's it, I am outta here." Jacob pulled out his crayons and construction paper and came up with plan so good the prisoners of Alcatraz could have escaped.

Step 1: Build a mannequin. He needed to put a dummy Jacob in the bed for his ever-worrying mother, who came to check on him at all hours of the night like a prison guard. So he took his largest stuffed bear. Dressed it in his pj's and tucked it under the covers. He stepped back and admired his work, stroking his chin like a villain who has a long and pointy beard.

Step 2: Put on a spy outfit. Jacob dug into the back of his closet and found a black turtleneck. He never thought this awful gift from his grandma would ever have any use, but for the first time he willingly put it on. He followed it up by putting on a pair of black jeans and a black hat. He admired himself in the mirror and turned the light off and had to quiet his laughter when he seemed to disappear in the darkened room.

Step 3: Supplies. Jacob took a pillowcase and filled it with everything he would need to survive. He chose his favorite action figures, a bag of Goldfish, a couple Fruit by the Foot, and a piggy bank (even though it was nearly empty).

With the preparations complete, Jacob waited until the cover of darkness to enact the final part of the plan and spent the last moments of daylight looking at his hand-drawn map of his house and of the backyard. He gazed at it expertly, like a master tactician in the war room, and finally picked up a red crayon and drew a thick streak from his window to the back gate—his predicted route to freedom.

The sun finally set and the escape began once he was sure his parents were safely enamored in the shows they routinely watched. He quietly lifted the window to his bedroom and looked over the ledge. On the other side, attached to the ledge, was the fire escape ladder his mom vehemently demanded be kept on the bedroom windows at all times. You can never be too safe, she would plead to her husband.

Within seconds he was out. His feet touched the cool grass below and he punched the air with excitement and did a little dance. Quickly he realized there was nothing to celebrate yet. Getting out of the room was the easy part and now Jacob looked into the great expanse of the backyard at night. "It looked a lot smaller on the map," he said under his breath.

In a dash, Jacob ran from the side of the house and dove onto the ground. He army-crawled through the enclosed backyard. He kept his body low and dragged himself as silently as he could. When his body gave way to exhaustion, he paused to regain his breath and looked up to see how far he had come. Within sight was his haven. There it was in all of its glory. A big wooden door, which on the other side carried all the freedom and candy a kid could hope for. The only thing that lay between him and certain fun was one more big run.

He looked back and saw he was about halfway there and far enough away that he didn't need to hide in the grass anymore. In one quick movement he jumped up and sprinted like a sprinting cat through the rest of the yard and dodged every hole and tree root sticking out of the ground from pure memory—the way only a child could—and jumped up the three stairs to the gate.

He took one last look back, saw the light of the TV erupting in the house and gave a cocky salute and stuck his tongue out and did a little dance of joy. There was no sign of movement inside the house and he could almost taste freedom. He pictured the endless supply of milkshakes and their creamy chill sliding down his throat, settling warmly into his stomach and imagined walking down the street with the enormous weight of the candy he'd keep in his pockets with no parents to tell him otherwise. At last it was time and Jacob decided to quit imagining and get to living. He put his hand onto the latch and his eyes widened and his mouth started to drool. He almost couldn't believe he made it. He threw his shoulder into the tall wooden gate and held back tears of joy.

Thud. Jacob pulled on the latch again and pushed himself into it again. *Thud.* It must be a pull door, he thought, and he heaved with all his might. It didn't budge.

Suddenly, the backyard lights flashed on with enormous intensity. It was like daylight under the night sky and Jacob stood like a startled deer in headlights. He was frozen in place and he couldn't see anything, but he heard the deep bellowing laughter of his dad. The lights began to dim and Jacob tracked the laughter to the sliding glass door and he saw his dad, standing proudly like a lion overlooking his pride, waving the mightiest of all weapons—the smart phone. A tool capable of controlling all the lights and Wi-Fi in his domain. In his other hand he held out and jingled the key to the lock on the gate.

Jacob fell to his knees. "I'm going to be grounded for sure."

Dreaming of revenge

The champagne pops and I watch as the bubbly drink drips down the bottle onto the carpet I just cleaned. Across the room I see people drag their vile shoes on a freshly polished hardwood floor. There is never a dull moment being a butler. In fact, there is rarely a fun moment either.

For many, being a butler is not a profession you choose. It is bestowed upon you and your dad and your granddad and your great granddad tell you "what an honor it is to serve such a great family for so many generations."

Bullocks, I say. It can be dressed up as much as one wants but I'd much rather be the person sitting in the soft-cushioned chair getting his shoes polished, not having to lift a finger—even for a sneeze. What honor is there in being the one doing the polishing and taking the abuse—both physical and mental—that comes with along with it? None, I say. There is no honor in being demeaned and dirtied for the sake of others.

I look around the old walls of this mansion, far too big for any family, and I see the shining armor of the glorious knights, the masterpiece sculptures with manly bodies like Adonis and womanly figures like Aphrodite, and the beautiful paintings with scenes of noble men with their fine jewelry, expensive clothes, and beautiful women. It's funny, there are more pieces of art than I can keep track of, but I can't help but notice there are no portraits of butlers or maids or gardeners in my master's abode. No sculptures of my lanky arms and rail-thin legs. No paintings of my pale skin, which sees no sun, and greasy hair that's washed in dirty water. There are no fortunes to be sought for the likes of help. No glory to be had. I have one ill-fitting suit, clunky shoes, and a wrinkled hat. Oh! I nearly forgot about my white cotton gloves. I have no time for a family and dating is out of the question. It is hard enough keeping track of my master's mistresses, let alone his wife.

On quiet days I like to think what it would be like if I were the master and he were the servant. Oh, what a heavenly thought indeed. With an iron fist I'd reign. My smile would be devilish. It would curl over ever so menacingly, like the Cheshire Cat, as I'd think up all the chores to be had. Nothing but the best, and then some, for me. I'd make him do the laundry twice, the dishes three times, and make the bed four times. With a tiny wire brush I'd make him scrape each and every brick up to the observatory clean.

Better yet I'd make him drive me to the country on the wettest, muddiest day. Just to have him turn back and wash the car and clean my boots. And when that is done, we'd go back out and do it all over again.

Oh, what a time I would have and the parties I'd throw. I'd invite the homeless to put on a show. I'd throw money from the balcony and watch them scrap over every penny. The papers would herald me as a generous fellow, a philanthropist, the best of the lot. I'd be on all the magazines and all over the TV, but really it would all be for a laugh. You couldn't go out without hearing of me. I would spread my wealth and pay the *real* people's tabs. They'd love me and I'd love them back. But not my master or his kind. They don't deserve my love. He would just have to sit in the cool, clammy basement and listen to the great times above him. Only when he is summoned would he be allowed to be seen. From there he could sweep all the broken glass and carry the leftover foods straight to the trash. From his hands and knees, I'd make him clean the stained carpet and pick up the shards of glass. Best yet, he'd have to sit in his filth afterwards until the grease and grime dripping from his clothes hardened and made him stiff. His body would be bruised and his spirit would be broken. Just then, when he thinks his night is done, I'd call for an inspection and chastise his appearance and ridicule him for embarrassing my family name. Maybe then he would learn.

Alas, it is but a dream. Instead I stand here in my grimy clothes, with a dirty cloth hanging off my shoulder as I try to wipe away the lipstick stain on a glass and smell the rotting food in the trash near my straw mattress. If only people knew what a mess my master would be without me. I don't think he knows right from left or how to tie a shoe. Don't even bother asking him to make a bed.

That's what they don't tell you in all the papers. These rich men, "sophisticated" they say. "True gentlemen," they applaud. Lies. They are nothing but a bunch of buffoons. Sure, they can take a picture and shake a hand but when it comes to the real stuff it is all the same. I'm not alone, either. Ask any butler or any maid, we all agree.

Maybe it was different in the past, when the families had to work for their status and wealth. But now inheritance has warped the mind. The separation of time and comfort has made their kind soft. They forget what it is like to be like me. These children and grandchildren have grown, but only in age. The silver spoon still sits in their mouth like a pacifier and their butts are cushioned, like a diaper, with money from every fall and scandal.

There is never a thanks or even a pleasant hello. That is all we ask for, really. A little acknowledgment would go a long way. Instead there is a snap of a finger and new job to do. Before you can take a breather, you hear your name called and there awaits another job piled on top of the rest. And I hate my name now. I curse my mother for naming me so. It makes my spine shiver like nails on a chalkboard by a shrieking cat.

But one day things will be different, and my dreams will come true, just wait and see. I will get my revenge. Don't worry, you'll see my name in the papers soon.

The search

The wind pushed its way through the trees, piercing into the man's coat and stiffening his body with each gust. His hand held onto the long shaft of an axe and he let it drag loosely in the snow behind him, allowing it to skip over the roots and rocks hidden beneath the tundra. He listened for the slightest sound as he peered into the never-ending abyss of a winter night, yet nothing joined the soft crunching of snow beneath his feet. As he moved deeper into the woods he began to feel uneasy. To be alone in such a vast land made the man feel small and the voice inside his head told him something must be wrong. Logic told him there must be something watching him. But he tried to shake it off. He was on a mission and he couldn't let the fear in the back of his mind stop him.

As the forest grew thicker the man stopped on occasion and inspected every limb and trunk around him. When he was truly impressed, he gave a tree or two a big shake. With a disappointing sigh he moved on and continued down the trail until something else caught his eye. Something that would make his town proud and happy to decorate. Before long he found himself miles from where he started, with no reward or ending in sight. The day was nearly over and the man considered turning back empty-handed before the uncomforting blanket of night fell onto the Earth. He thought of the warm fire crackling as he sipped a warm drink, his dog lying on his frozen feet, and a good book in hand.

He shook those thoughts away almost as soon as they came and he cursed his selfishness. He had people, a whole town full of them, who relied on him and he had his code to live by. As he reminded his friends and family often, if you say you will do something, you do it. Soon his thoughts wandered off again and he was flooded with images of the children's tears falling down their cheeks like a waterfall and their mumbling words as they tried to speak through the sadness. And then he pictured their parents and the shop owners he visited daily and the words they would say behind his back. It was then he turned his body away from the direction of home and pressed on.

The gusts of wind froze his lungs and he gasped and panted on a hike up a hill and through the crippling snow that was rapidly approaching his knees in height. The hill was much bigger than he remembered but he pictured the children's joyous faces from last year as he dragged the mighty tree into the center of town and how he held them on their shoulders so they could put their favorite ornament on the branches. So he pushed onwards and kept on going until he screamed in pain, eventually falling to all fours in the chilling snow. He crawled to a big tree and his back hit the trunk with a thud and the birds busted out of the trees, shocking the man to his core. Chuckling, he gathered himself and sat pondering while clouds of breath poured out of his mouth.

A little bit further, that's where it is, he told himself. It must be somewhere close. He swung the axe atop his shoulder and pushed himself off the tree and back to the hunt. Again he stopped and inspected the trees around him. The trail seemed untouched to even the bravest creatures and with a quick glance he noticed he was out of sight from the light of his home. The trees grew larger and snow grew deeper and he moved slower, but he forced himself to go on. He looked ahead and stood tall in the face of the final rays of sunshine and watched the big yellow disk take a final bow on this day. It was now or never. The man held his axe in front of him and spun in a circle with his eyes closed. His axe was pointing at the broad trunk of a tree when he stopped and opened his eyes and he nodded his head. He managed to give off a smile through his frozen face and strode towards it. He gave it a final inspection and a shove and it didn't budge. "*Aha,*" his booming voice called out in celebration. This was the one.

He rose his weapon in both his hands and swung the mighty axe, tearing into the tree, jamming it into the now-splintered bark. With a heave he ripped it from the trunk and swung again. The tree creaked and cracked and was joined by another thud of the axe.

He held himself up on his knees and stared at his work and wiped the almost-frozen sweat off his brow. The man's head shook in astonishment at the size of the tree and what he thought wasn't even a dent in its side. He brought the axe clear above his head and forced it down on the trunk again and again. Mustering his strength, he swung one last time and finally it broke through to the other side. He stood back and leaned his weight on the axe with an oozing confidence and listened to the last pieces of wood give way. "Timber," he yelled out to the empty world and with a smile on his face he watched the tree fall, landing softly into the snow as if it were a pillow.

He pulled a bunch of rope from his coat and methodically strapped it around the trunk of the tree and fastened it to himself like a harness and looked back into the void. The stars were shining bright in the night sky and he looked up and found the Belt of Orion. "Onward to home," he whispered to himself. His body was worn and tired and the weight of the tree was nearly too much, but he knew home was on the other side of this ordeal. He kept his eye on the stars and let Orion guide him home and let the faces of the children smiling and the townspeople's proud nods of approval fill his thoughts. Now he welcomed the thoughts of the crackling fire and his dog and for the first time this day he didn't feel alone.

Tale of the piano player

Alfred glanced up from his piano and his eyes were drawn to an apple sitting in front of him. His stomach sank and he began to shake and hit the wrong keys.

The crowd grew silent and turned to the little man in the corner and looked at him with disgust.

"Uh . . . sorry . . . everyone, I'm taking five."

Alfred stood up. His suit was a size too big, wrinkled, and covered in dust. He looked out to the crowd, seemingly waiting for someone to give him permission to walk away. Nobody gave him a second of their time.

Alfred put his head down and quickly walked into the back of the bar, climbed over the boxes of beer and liquor, and found his way to the emergency exit to the alley.

"Going somewhere, Alfie?"

His skin turned white and he took a big gulp before turning around to see a man towering over him.

"Ma . . . ma . . . ma . . . me?" Alfred forced out.

The massive man in a pinstripe suit lit a cigarette, momentarily showing off his brutish face with a smile. "You saw the boss's calling card, didn't yah?"

Alfred tried to back up but ran into the wall. His hands became clammy and he pushed up his Coke-bottle glasses.

He thought back to that fateful moment when he saw the apple.

"I was just on my way to see him."

"Lucky for you then, I'm here to give you a ride," the brutish man said.

He reached for Alfred and lifted him by the arm and pushed him through the door, his shoes dragging across the floor.

Sitting in the alley was a jet-black Ford Model 18 with its engine running.

Before Alfred had a chance to whine he was gagged and a bag was thrown over his head. He then felt himself get tossed into the car.

He could hardly make out a voice as the three men in the car argued over baseball, women, and the strongest of the bunch.

"Whatta yah think, Alfie?" a voice called out. The men laughed, knowing he couldn't answer with a sock stuffed down his throat.

"It's gonna be alright Alfie, the boss just wants to talk, that's all." The car erupted in laughter. "He musta missed yah and your pathetic face."

After fifteen minutes of harassment and stomach-turning driving, the car came to an abrupt halt and the smell of rotting fish filled Alfred's nose. Simultaneously, the car's doors opened and closed. A forceful tug threw him from the car and he gave out a muffled scream as he hit the wet pavement.

"Have some respect for yah self. Get up. You're gonna see the boss looking like that?"

The goons picked him up and dusted him off, being sure to give him a few cheap punches to the gut before ripping off the bag and tearing the sock out of his mouth.

Alfred took a big gasp of air and tried to take a look around as he was shoved through a warehouse door.

"Wait here," the brutish man from the piano bar snapped.

An agonizing amount of time went by. Alfred stood alone in a poorly lit room with only his thoughts.

"Why, oh why, why, why. I thought I was off the hook," Alfred whispered to himself. "How did they find me?"

He fell to his knees and broke into tears. He wiped the blood off his face and cleaned his glasses the best he could. One lens was cracked, and his suit was so dirty the other lens became smudged with a mixture of dirt, blood, and the usual filth found on Alfred's suit.

A door opened with a deafening creak and the brutish man pulled Alfred up to his feet.

"He's ready for you."

Alfred, for once, was gently walked into an out-of-place room.

Bookshelves sprawled the walls and a large wooden desk sat at the center of the room. On it sat photos of people he couldn't quite make out. There was a picture window that gave way to a view of the river. It was eerily quiet. The only sound was the ticking of a clock that sat on the desk.

A man with silver hair was looking out the window before turning around to greet Alfred.

"Ah, Alfred, my boy," a grizzled voice called out. "I hope you had a pleasant journey."

The brutish man snickered and gave Alfred a jab to the gut, signaling him to answer.

"They were great, sir," Alfred whimpered. "Top-notch service as always."

The man put his glass of whiskey down on the table and pulled out a massive leather chair and took a seat. A bowl of apples was placed just under the tabletop light and he reached for one. The rings on his fingers glistened. Alfred couldn't help but be awestruck at the size of the diamonds and the amount of gold one hand could carry.

"Leave us," the boss said to the brutish man.

"Now, Alfred, you know why you're here don't you? I take it you received my card," he said while taking a bite out of the apple. "You tried to run away before your debt was paid, Alfred. That doesn't make me a happy man."

"Sir."

"Don't interrupt me, Alfred. That's rude. Like I was saying, you tried to run away. You've got balls, I'll give you that. However, you forget whose city this is. You can't hide from me. The good news, you'll be free and clear after tonight."

Alfred looked at him in a stunned silence. Thoughts raced through his head but he couldn't come up with a coherent sentence. Instead he just stood with his mouth open.

"You do this job for me and we'll call it even," the boss said. "Now this is what you gotta do."

Alfred listened to the boss tell him about another man, a rival of his who owed him a favor.

"Unfortunately for him, I don't like him as much as you. You, Alfred, lost me a lot of money but I can't say I'm surprised. Just look at you. You are a pathetic excuse for a man. You couldn't even run your own joint and now you're back playing piano for a two-bit tip on a Monday. Maybe it was my fault for feeling bad for you."

"I don't know what to say, sir. I tried my best."

"Your best? Ha. You call that your best. You better do your best tonight or it's gonna be a long night for you. Now get outta my office, the sight of you makes me sick."

Alfred walked out of the room and was met with a big, gold-toothed smile.

"Ready, partner?" the brutish man said, chuckling.

Alfred and the man got back into the car and sped their way downtown to the financial district.

Alfred started to shake, his palms began to sweat again and he curled up into a ball in the passenger seat.

"Come on, Alfie, what you so scared about? All you gotta do is play the piano like you always do, but this time plant this little number inside."

Alfred glanced up at a bomb and began to sob.

The two walked up to a large metal door and the brutish man knocked.

"I got your piano player here, let us in."

The door swung open and jazz music exploded from the inside.

"This the guy, you serious?" the doorman said.

"Trust me, he will blow you away."

Alfred walked down the steps like a dog with his tail between his legs and a bomb in his pocket. He moved his way up to the piano and took a seat. He took a look at the crowd and noticed dozens of sharply dressed men, puffing away at cigars and eyeing the waitresses in their pencil skirts.

His hands shook as the jazz band moved offstage. A rare silence came over the bar.

"What you waiting for?" a voice cried out.

"Sorry," Alfred stuttered into the mic. After a few missed keys Alfred felt back at home, his peaceful place behind a piano.

Song after song went by and soon enough Alfred forgot about all his troubles and his deal with the boss and the bomb in his pocket.

His eyes shot open.

The bomb.

Sitting in his coat pocket on the piano bench sat a bomb raring to go off when the night was done. His job was to get in, play a few songs, and get out. Hours must have gone by and the bomb was still ticking away, ready to blow whether he was in the building or not.

Alfred stopped abruptly to the dismay of the crowd.

"Hey, what's the idea?" a few men shouted.

"Uh, I gotta get a drink," Alfred nervously spoke into the mic. "Give me ten minutes and I'll be back playing."

Alfred pulled a watch out of his pocket and gave it a look. He let out a relieved sigh. He still had an hour until the explosion.

Now to get out of this place, Alfred thought. He searched all over for the brutish man, but he was nowhere to be found. He started to ask the bartender, then the waitress, and even the doorman for any sign. But nobody had a clue.

A fire in Alfred grew.

Alfred walked into the kitchen and took a quick glance before grabbing a steak knife off the table. He slid it down his sock and held it steady in his shoe.

Before anyone found him out, he ran out the back door and tried to make his way back to the boss. He barely remembered leaving in his nervous state and didn't think to look around. The only thing he remembered was the fishy smell when he was gagged and thrown in the backseat of the car.

Alfred started down the street and before he turned the corner the night sky lit up and an explosion rang in his ears.

He turned around to see debris flying through the air and smoke billowing up to the night sky.

Anxiety filled him and he broke out into a panicked run before being grabbed and thrown into an alley.

"Well damn, Alfie," a familiar voice called out. "I would have never bet you made it out of there alive."

"I thought you abandoned me," he said, pushing the towering man. "We have to get out of here. They are going to know it was us. The police will be coming."

"Whoa, whoa, whoa, just wait a second. You weren't supposed to make it out of there, Alfie."

The brutish man lunged towards him and Alfred pulled the steak knife out of his sock and held it out in front of the falling man, stabbing him right in his belly.

"You . . . you son of a bitch. You stabbed me."

Alfred fell to his knees and began to cry. "I didn't mean it. You were coming at me. I didn't mean it."

Alfred watched the man die and looked at his blood-soaked hands. His gut instinct told him to run, so he got up and ran, passing by the car his dead captor had been using.

He jumped in and sped off and drove for the nearest highway. He nervously looked into the rearview mirror at every car that tailed him.

After fifteen minutes of driving the car spurted to a stop and died on the highway, just outside of the city proper.

Alfred ran, holding his thumb out, praying for any friendly car to pull over and take him further out of the city. It was to no avail. He fled for the nearest exit and made his way down the off ramp.

He found himself in a little suburban town just outside of the city and read a sign at a stoplight.

POLICE: ONE MILE EAST

Exhausted, Alfred mustered up any remaining strength to continue for the only salvation he could think of.

He could explain it all. The police will understand the truth, he thought. Being abducted, fearing his life unless he listened to the boss. He'd tell him he didn't know about the bomb, that he stabbed that man and stole the car in self-defense. He'd even try to take them to the boss and get him thrown in jail if he had to.

It will be fine, he told himself with every step he took towards the police department.

The front doors swung open and Alfred stumbled inside the building and headed towards the front desk.

"I didn't do it . . . I didn't do it . . . I need help, they are after me. The explosion, the knife, the stolen car . . . it wasn't my fault," Alfred rambled before collapsing to the floor and passing out.

Alfred woke up in the hospital with the sun beating down on his face. He strained to move. His body was wrapped in bandages from the night's events. He looked around but he was practically blind without his glasses. He recognized the sounds and knew he was in a hospital and under the protection of doctors and nurses. He felt at ease and safe for the first time since his debacle started.

"I did it, I got away."

Alfred sighed and reached out for his glasses on the nightstand and struggled to put them on. He adjusted to the bright hospital lights and took a look around the hospital room.

Alfred grabbed the rails of his bed, his knuckles turned white. His heart rate monitor went off and he screamed for a nurse, a doctor, anyone to come help him.

Sitting on the chair in front of him was a fresh apple.

Our friend the machine

Richard was hardly awake when the clock struck 9:00 a.m. but still he was poured out of the bed that was promptly made thereafter. From there he was clothed and carried to the bathroom where the machine conveniently shaved his face and brushed his teeth before sending him off to the kitchen, where a fresh cup of coffee and buttered toast sat perfectly centered on the table in front of the sole chair.

He squirmed as his feet were taken from under him, but he fell gently into the seat, as he did every morning. A TV jolted on to the daily news and hovered in front of him, but Richard ignored it. It is hardly news if it never changed. Everything was perfect. The world's crises were solved long ago. No longer were there humanitarian problems, or wars, or political scandals. The Machine, as it came to be known, made sure of that. It was "the last thing you'll ever need, or want, again" the advertisement always said. And now mankind enjoyed its pampered lifestyle and chose not to lift a finger. It was better this way, they claimed. The less men, women, and children did, the less problems there could be.

Before his empty cup could touch the table, it was refilled and Richard rolled his eyes but took a much-needed sip. It trickled down his throat and settled into his stomach, warming him as it went. It was one of the few signs that told him he was alive. Within moments the kitchen looked as though it was on the showroom floor and all evidence of anyone being there was wiped away. The clock struck 9:30 and Richard was moved to the front door and his coat was draped on.

"I think it will be a cold day, Richard," a robotic voice called out.

Richard looked out the window and to the sky and saw the beaming sun get covered by a sudden pack of clouds. The street was covered in shade and the temperature gauge plummeted from seventy-five degrees to sixty-five. It was perfect weather for traveling. A perfect Midwestern winter at that. Not too hot, not too cold, and not a sign of storms in the forecast.

"Well, who woulda thought? It was right," he said.

A certain frustration could be heard in Richard's voice and he clenched his fist. The door opened for him and he stepped outside and gazed at the picket fences, the perfectly manicured lawns and the cookie-cutter houses that lined the street for miles. The roads were jet-black and contrasted wonderfully with the white vinyl sidings of the two-story homes. The smooth streets were lined with egg-shaped autonomous vehicles that moved like a merry-go-round. Each pod was spaced out to the nanometer, traveled at the same constant speed, and only broke the tight formation when someone was ready to enter one and even then, it was a seamless action.

The sight of it began to make Richard sick and he decided to walk. However, an alarm went off and a robotic voice echoed in the street.

"Please enter a vehicle. Please enter a vehicle. We wouldn't want you getting tired."

Richard's brow furrowed and he rubbed his temples. He muttered to himself while grinding his teeth but listened to the command and moved to the sidewalk where an egg-shaped pod met him and opened its bay door. The seats contoured to his body and moved in a way to give him full range of motion and enough room to sleep and take a three-course meal.

"To work," he said.

After work dinner was made and the dishes were cleaned. The TV turned to his favorite channel and his feet were massaged, in case he got sore from his morning incident, and he was dressed in his freshly washed pajamas. The machine poured him a drink and he took his night cap in a familiar anger.

The next morning he was poured out of bed. His teeth were cleaned, his face shaved, and in the kitchen a slice of toast and a cup of coffee awaited him, and the TV turned to the news. And at night dinner was made and his clothes were washed, and his favorite show was on TV. And this happened the next day and the day after that. Before long weeks went by and then months. For decades Richard, and the rest of the world, lived this so-called life and he had to reach to the deepest memories to remember a time without the machine.

On one occasion, while the machine took care of his morning routine, he looked at himself in the mirror. His skin was pale, in a sickly way, and his arms were like bare tree branches in the dead of winter. His chest was sunken in and shoulders hunched over. He didn't recognize the man looking back at him when he met the reflection of his eyes.

They were sad and the gleam of a lively middle-aged man was long disappeared. The sight of himself sparked a feeling he once remembered, and it boiled over into a violent chop towards the robotic arm brushing his teeth. He spat the remaining toothpaste on the ground and ran his hands under the faucet, feeling the warm water run on his hands and let it cascade over his fingers before throwing it onto his face and letting it drip onto his shirt with little care.

Richard then rushed out of the room and ran past the kitchen, ignoring the cup of coffee and toast and the pleading voice saying his breakfast will get cold, and to a seldom-used door, the almost-forgotten one that led to a now-defunct basement.

The old wood steps creaked as he slowly moved down. Each step was like walking for the first time and he wondered how long it had been since he walked down a set of stairs manually. The dirt and dust hung heavy in the air and was like walking in a fog. Due to the lack of attention, and need, the basement was more of a junkyard. When the Machine was installed into homes, it was hooked up to a new grid system. One that citizens had no access to. The laundry machines sat unused and rusting, along with detached fuse boxes, heaters, and any other mechanical/electric appliance or tool and outlets younger generations wouldn't even recognize. Mops sat in dirty water and crusty towels hung from a clothesline that lost all of its tautness. It was a ghastly sight Richard wished to never see again, but the monotony and sense of uselessness overcame him and he needed to feel alive again. This time a sip of coffee wasn't enough. He soon found his way to a shadowy corner of the room and rested his eyes on a faded red trunk. Its leather straps shattered as he pulled at them and its rusty hinges creaked, breaking the silence.

The aroma spewing out of the inside of the trunk flooded his nose and sent him decades worth of memories. He glanced at trinkets, books, and old toys from when he was a boy but tossed them all aside. It wasn't until he pulled out a simple metal toolbox that he took any real time to examine the contents. He fiddled with the screws inside and pulled on the tape measure and flipped the screwdrivers in the air and caught them. Then he found the wooden handle of a five-pound hammer. Tears rolled down his cheeks while Richard held it delicately in his hand. They were once grizzled and he used to grip the handle mightily, remembering how it was an extension of the man's hand.

Now he could hardly lift it without shaking. He felt like an infant and the hammer felt foreign to him while it sat loosely—no matter how hard he gripped—in his now-dainty hand.

Something in the bottom of the toolbox caught Richard's eye and he reached for it. It was an old photograph, a Polaroid, that was beginning to fade but he could make out two clear-cut bodies. Both were dressed in tight-fitting button-up shirts, due to their muscular physique, worn blue jeans and had leather tool bags hanging from the waist. Behind them was a hand-built house. The label was written in black permanent marker and simply said *The carpenter and his apprentice.*

He began swinging the hammer, but it forced him off-balance and with a crash the tool fell to the ground. Richard wiped the tears from his face and rubbed his thumb over the face of his father. A fire sparked deep in Richard and he told himself this was the beginning of a new day. He made the basement his new sanctuary and began to workout. He did a few handfuls of push-ups and sit-ups and thought it would be best to return upstairs.

Back in the kitchen the machine asked him if he was OK and it brought him a glass of water and medication, stating that his heart rate was elevated and he was sweating. Richard detested answering to the machine and having to ask permission for things, but he figured it was the only way to stop any red flags from popping up in the machine's computations. So he asked to add a two-hour block of personal time, uninterrupted, and an order of basic free weight equipment.

There was an eerie silence, and Richard could almost hear the machine coming up with the possible outcomes of the request. After what felt like hours, the machine complied.

"That is an acceptable request. Order for Richard will arrive in three hours and eight minutes," it said.

Richard felt like a kid on Christmas when the machine brought in the order. He explored each and every weight and pully and checked to see how much cushion the bench had—it was satisfactory. The machine put it all together in a matter of minutes and rearranged a living space to accommodate the equipment.

For weeks Richard used up every two-hour block allocated for the gym. The strenuous life healed him. He could feel his strength returning to him, the color returning to his skin, and a general confidence that came from feeling good about yourself. He could also feel the cold stare of the machine watching him. After a few days of showing results he knew he had to trick the machine, much like a child trying to fake sick to his mother. In both examples some things were easier said than done. He would fumble glasses, pretending to struggle to lift them and spill the drink or just drop the glass on the ground. On other occasions he'd stumble around and look weak and sickly. It seemed to work, but he couldn't shake the feeling of being watched. So, when he could, he escaped to the basement and used remnants of the past to build his future.

Though they didn't work, the junkyard of appliances proved to be useful. As they say, one man's trash is another man's treasure. While he had the gym upstairs to work his body, he had the appliances to work his mind. He was able rewire components, tie knots recalled from the scout handbook found in his trunk, and remember the other skills a boy learned from his father. Soon his hands could feel the wood again and the tools felt comfortable. He challenged himself and found a broken piece of wood laying in the dust and whittled it down to a small arrowhead, which he turned into a necklace with twine rope, now hanging from his neck. It was a simple shape but weeks ago it would have been impossible to create or even picture within the broken two-by-four.

Each morning there was a glint in his eye as he looked at himself in the mirror. A cloud of darkness was lifted and under it he found his courage lurking and brought it to the light. It was only then that the man was ready to face his adversary. Richard headed towards his sanctuary but found the old wooden door was installed with a flashy chrome lock.

"What's this about?"

"Scans show it is unsafe beyond this point. Unauthorized citizens are restricted from entering."

Richard fought back. He would no longer succumb to the machine.

"Unsafe? What is unsafe? It is an obsolete cellar, full of dust."

"Access denied."

"I want to go on a trip," he said. "Order camping supplies and transportation to the woods."

The hum of the machine was louder than Richard remembered, and he grinned. It was nervous now.

"Request denied."

Richard scoffed. "And why is that?"

"Activity deemed too dangerous."

"Maybe to you."

The machine hummed and didn't respond. Richard knew it was calculating and chose now to take action. He threw himself forward into the basement door and crashed into the hollow door, shattering it as he went past and down the stairs. A robotic arm rushed after Richard as he hopped down the stairs. A light flashed on from its three-pronged claw and lit up the dusty room.

Richard was at his trunk, arming himself with his old tools. Before long he spun around and swung his heavy hammer. There was a thunderous clank and it echoed between his ears like a gunshot. The arm flailed to the ground and Richard quickly reacted by stepping on the claw, pushing a sharpened chisel into the machine, and slammed the hammer on top of the tool. It fell deep into the machine and sparks cracked and buzzed as the wires snapped apart and burned.

He wanted to spend more time looking at the crippled arm of the machine but knew he couldn't let his pride get the best of him. It was just the beginning. Richard trekked back upstairs with his hammer in tow and pulled the rusty hatchet from between his belt and jeans. With brute force he came down with the tools onto the tables and chairs and mirrors and walls. He took down the counters and waited for retaliation that was bound to come.

The floor jolted and swayed back and forth and shook him off-balance. Arms shot out of the ceiling and the floor moved him into striking distance. He was on the machine's home field and though he didn't want to admit it, it was in control.

"Attention, attention. Cease and desist."

Richard rose to his feet in defiance. He puffed out his chest and held the hatchet high over his head. The machine quickly disarmed him. It thrust its claw into his bicep and squeezed it until Richard let out an ugly scream. He fell back to his knees and looked around. He had to get out. The only way to beat the machine was to leave. To be noticed, to make a scene, was the only way to garner attention and ultimately win. For one man's actions could speak to the hearts of thousands.

In a flash the hammer was flying through the air and it crashed through the window. He followed and jumped for freedom. He tasted the dirt. The blood rushed to his head and he tried to move, but his leg was caught by the machine. He rasped for the green grass inches from his face and dug his fingers into the ground and clawed his way from the pull of the machine. The ground gave way and he was left with chunks of earth and broken glass in his hands.

By now eyes from neighbors could be seen peeking through their blinds and alarms began to ring out up and down the street like the wail of a tornado siren. Richard felt their glares and it made him grin. The show must go on, he told himself, and he grabbed the hammer from the yard. The wooden shaft of the hammer was soon drenched in blood, but he ignored the pain and turned to swing at the arm holding him back. The arm twisted and turned while evading the heaving motions. On occasion Richard struck himself and cried out. His ankle was shattered. From the machine or the hammer's blows one could not be sure, but he used it to his advantage and was able to slip away from the arm's grip.

Richard tried to stand. He leaped up and immediately fell down. He flailed forward like a fish out of water and did what he could and tried to get to the street and in view of the public.

"Remember, my friends. Remember how it used to be. To be free. To think for yourself. To do what you want when you want to. Remember how it felt to go for a joyride, or swim in the lake, or just sleep in and do nothing. Find your courage. It is there hidden from you. They can't take what doesn't belong to them, they never could. They could only beat you down and make you feel weak and feeble. Now is the time to stand up for your rights. To stand up for your freedom and take our world back. We are what makes this world, not the machine."

Richard pleaded from his knees and looked at the monochromatic houses and could see them being put into a lockdown mode. The shutters slammed shut and the locks on the doors rang out as they were turned into the lock position. The pods of cars parted out of the way and Richard watched a long, dark black vehicle speed towards him. It screeched to a stop in front of him and the double doors swung open and all that could be seen was darkness.

He wiped the blood from his mouth and stood up valiantly. He puffed out his chest and held his head up high. It was the last time Richard was seen.

Within hours the beat-up house was repaired and from the outside. It was as though nothing happened. But inside there were murmurs and people began to take long looks in the mirror.

Acknowledgments

There is an endless amount of people who deserve thanks for this book. It is truly impossible to take on such as task without the love and support from those around you. From every teacher I've had, to my friends and family, and to every passing character along the way, I say thank you. You have all impacted me, inspired me, and drove me to not only complete this book, but help me realize it was possible.

A special thank you goes out to my beautiful wife, Savannah. I truly couldn't have, and wouldn't have, done this without you. I thank you for the hours spent listening to my ramblings and talking through ideas with me and for reading every single word I have ever written. And I thank you for reading those same words over, and over, and over again.